Arise, You Rebel Angels

Mary Trepanier

Published by Cwtch Press, Redmond, WA 98052

Cover design by Mariah Sinclair

E-book ISBN: 978-1-947234-34-5

Print ISBN: 978-1-947234-35-2

10 9 8 7 6 5 4 3 2 1

Trigger Warning: Graphically violent scenes in this book might be disturbing to some. The material is not appropriate for people under age 18.

ARISE, YOU REBEL ANGELS

Book 4 of Tales of the End Times

MARY TREPANIER

Chapter 1

*H*is back against the iron railing of a hotel balcony, Pete glowed red-gold with the aura of a god. He punched Mark in the face.

The older man head-butted him, hard.

They fell over the railing.

Just before they hit, twelve floors down, Joanie jolted awake.

She sat up, wrapping her arms around herself. An ocean of sorrow filled her, tight and painful in her chest and throat.

Her control broke, and the tears fell down.

It was all her fault.

Nearly a year had passed since her boyfriend Pete had saved her from her client Mark's attack. But her dreams recalled it like yesterday.

Early-morning winter sun streamed through her windows. Across them, a grapevine climbed a trellis, brown twisting arms leafless. Vine shadows draped across the quilt on her bed. The sunlight hinted at life.

Maybe she could go back to sleep.

Another early morning dawned, the sky pale peach over a stand of fir trees. It looked like the Northwest.

In the dream, this was her farm.

In a high-ceilinged room, a woodstove banished a seeping chill. Filmy polyester curtains were tied back to show dawn over the gardens. Nearby on the flagged patio lay containers of herbs—rosemary, sage, thyme. A few apple trees, past them, marked the edge of an orchard.

Joanie stepped out French doors to frozen mist hanging pink among the trees. It calmed her to stand there, greeting morning.

Waking again, she wondered if her future self had sent the dream to tempt her forward. In the future, maybe she'd still be full of grief, but she and her friends had escaped and made a farm.

Chapter 2

The coven held ritual at Hannah's house, which stood behind a rose trellis on a side street in North Seattle. At the first full moon of the year, early January, despite the cold, they planned to circle by the fire basket in the backyard.

Huddled in her peacoat, Joanie bussed there from the Seattle University District coffee shop she helped manage. She'd picked up accounting classes, was going for a second bachelor's. In a real way, her vocation was worshipping Inanna—sex work, but with the aim of healing and love—but she hadn't done that for a long time. She wasn't in a good place to. She maintained her erotic fan site; that was about it.

She leaned her cheek against the cold metal of the interior bus wall, letting her brunette hair cascade to screen her face.

She hadn't expected Pete's death to still haunt her. Sometimes the memories lulled, but then she'd see some bit of news and want to talk to him about it, or hear a song he'd played her.

Tears threatened, but she pushed them down.

When she got to the house, she found the coven in the basement for preritual discussion. They'd settled across a couple of couches and the floor, under a Celtic tree of life hanging.

"Before we get started," Hannah said, "Nora's taking people for her poison path course, and she wanted to check if anyone was interested."

One of the newer coven members raised her hand. "What's the poison path?"

"It's the study of poisonous plants you can use as medicines—for example, flying-ointment plants like belladonna."

"I'm interested, if I can make the timing work," Joanie said.

Keeping busy helped stave off her grief over Pete. The idea of working with growing things evoked her recurring farm dreams—orchards, herb gardens, plots of greens where her community raised what they could, a margin of resilience against the future.

"Anyone else?"

Alyssa raised her hand shyly. "Maybe. I need to check my class schedule." This past six months or so, consulting with Hannah, Alyssa had focused on mystical work with a spirit named Moonshadow, linked to the moon's dark.

Beside Alyssa, stroking her white-blonde hair, sat her boyfriend Gus. Small and wiry, he wore his dark hair a bit long, growing out a bleached streak. He was still finishing his biology degree.

Over time, Joanie had come to trust him, although a couple years before he'd broken off a relationship with a man who was a white supremacist. Max, leader of the far-right ritual group Odin's Hunt, believed in "esoteric traditionalism" and violence, and he'd taken that belief far enough a man had died. A year later, right after Pete's death, a new threat had arrived from that quarter, or so they suspected—Joanie had gotten email accusing her of having Pete kill Mark. Nothing had appeared since.

"Tonight, I wanted to bring in a practice I learned from another group," Hannah said. "A lot of traditional witches trace lineage back to the Watcher angels and their children, mentioned in the Bible and the apocryphal Book of Enoch. The Watchers are fallen angels who mated with the children of Adam and Eve. For that, they were punished. Their leader Samyaza hanged himself from the constellation Orion in repentance."

"I don't see what this has to do with our practice," Joanie said.

Hints of Christianity in witchcraft made her twitch. Her mother had fallen prey to a toxic form of that religion.

Hannah gave Joanie a quelling look over her reading glasses.

"We've talked about this before. Some of our forebears had to hide their spellwork in Christianity. But angels aren't just Christian or Jewish—Hekate has been called the Queen of the Angels. You work with Inanna, who's syncretized with Ishtar. There's a later myth of Samyaza losing the name of God to a maiden called Istahar, sorta like Inanna getting Enki drunk and stealing the rules of governance. The early Jewish tribes were part of the whole broad culture of the

Near East, and some of their myths connect to other peoples there."

"Fine." She sat back into her girlfriend Cleo's arms. Coveners could present the rituals they wanted, within reason, and Hannah was high priestess. She and Hannah could hash it out later.

"To start, I want to acknowledge a goddess I honor in my personal work. That's the Star Mother of Feri Tradition, whom the Feri call God Hirself. She's the living immanent universe, the end and beginning of all."

They gathered their coats and trooped outside.

In the black night, the small yard lay encircled in leafless trees, branches reaching upward to translucent sky.

They had started late, on purpose, around midnight. The moon stood directly overhead, beside Orion, breasting through the milky light. Rigel, blue and bright, shone at the constellation's corner.

"We work below Orion to honor Samyaza's sacrifice."

Hannah cut the circle, acknowledged the Star Mother, and read excerpts from the Book of Enoch.

Joanie zoned out. When she was confronted with Judeo-Christian text, a self-protection layer came up. But some verses made her listen harder.

"After the children of men had increased in those days, beautiful and comely daughters were born to them. And the angels, the sons of heaven, saw and lusted after them, and said one to another: 'Behold, we will choose for ourselves wives from among the children of men, and beget ourselves children.'"

The fire glinted on Hannah's glasses. "Tradition says they went with men, too."

She continued, "Azazel taught mankind to make swords and knives and shields and coats of mail, and taught them to see what was behind them—mirrors, in other words—and to make works of art: bracelets and ornaments, and the use of rouge, and the beautifying of the eyebrows, and the choicest stones and all coloring substances and the metals of the earth. And there was great wickedness and fornication."

"Yay, fornication!" Joanie whispered. Cleo snickered. "Coming to Earth because you're down to fuck? How cool is that?"

"I like a fallen angel who teaches about swords and makeup."

"Men cried aloud in their destruction, and their voices reached heaven. Michael and Gabriel and other angels looked down and saw the great amount of blood spilled on the earth, and all the wickedness committed. And they spoke to their Lord, the King."

Hannah closed the book, using her finger as a bookmark.

"I'm skipping a bit here, but God is pissed. He orders the Flood to kill the Watchers' children. And there's more."

She opened the book again, flipping pages. "He tells the other angels: 'Bind Azazel hand and foot, and put him in darkness; make an opening in the desert, in Dudael, and put him there.' Then, a bit later: 'Announce to Samyaza and to the others who are with him, when all their sons shall have slain one another, bind them under the hills of the earth for seventy generations, till the day of their judgment. They will be led to the abyss of fire; in torture and in prison they will be locked for all eternity.' The Watcher angels cried and repented, or at least some did, but the Lord stuck with the plan."

"Shit," Joanie said. "In hell for all eternity."

She hadn't missed this part of Christianity. She'd been trapped herself, by zealots in her family.

"Maybe not forever," Cleo said. "Seventy generations are probably over by now."

"In honor of the Watchers," Hannah said, "we offer to the fire."

She poured incense and wine onto the flames. With a hiss, the fire leapt. Another covener set food offerings on the logs.

The fire crackled in frosty darkness, the citrus scent of blonde frankincense rising from the flames. Against the cold, Joanie burrowed under Cleo's arm, and Cleo hugged her briefly, releasing her own aura of sandalwood.

"It's a little cold to meditate outside tonight. But before we go in, let's stand a few moments in silence as our offerings burn, and give thanks to our fallen angel ancestors. As a focus, look at Orion, where some say Samyaza still hangs."

Stepping away from Cleo, Joanie focused on the stars.

Icy blue Rigel stared at her. Around her she felt the Watcher company, hundreds of dark forms. In some places, gold flickered in firelight, as against a breastplate or sword belt—she imagined the fallen angels armed.

Then someone was in her space, crowding her, a burly male form.

"Hello." A low-pitched voice. "Imagine your being here."

She rocked backward a step. "Do I know you?"

"From a long time ago."

With a scent of burned garlic, the spirit disappeared. A black feather drifted past her to the ground.

Chapter 3

*P*uabi-Ekur, the incubus-succubus who was Joanie's spirit guide, monitored her from a half-step away on the astral. When they felt a yank on the psychic line, they jumped in.

At Puabi-Ekur's approach, the spirit visitor popped out of Joanie's space and disappeared. Puabi-Ekur noticed burned garlic, a component of the coven's Hekate incense. Perhaps the Lady had come to protect Joanie.

With a ripple of color, the scene shifted. Puabi-Ekur was drawn up and out, as they'd been before by Hekate Soteira—not to the starry heaven they associated with the goddess, but to a new space. This was an earthly place, perhaps a pocket universe.

It felt familiar. In a desert, an oasis, it brought back their lives in ancient Sumer. The horizon lay fuzzy; the brown dusty line of earth verged into the dark-blue sky of twilight. Palm leaves whispered in a breeze. All of it raised a longing for the past.

From that horizon advanced a shadow, which became a form: male, in armor, with dark-olive skin, a warrior's muscles, long, black, curling hair, and full well-curved lips. His face was almost too beautiful for a man. He was clean-shaven, his eyes lined with kohl.

His kilt was studded leather, above it a bronze breast-plate—from Babylon, near Puabi-Ekur's city, but later in time. Slung from his shoulder harness hung a sheathed sword.

In response, by instinct, Puabi-Ekur presented them-selves as Puabi, the dancer of Uruk. With crimped brunette hair, frame slender but wide-hipped, she wore a costume covered with silver coins.

The warrior drew close. On his back flared a pair of black-feathered wings, a head taller than he was. A breeze traveled with him, fluttering his feathers. His eyes were grey-blue, the color of blue topaz.

"Greetings, most fair," he said.

"Who are you?"

Pale eyes scanned Puabi, pausing a moment on her breasts, her mouth.

"I am called many things. You may call me Azazel. And yourself?"

"Why are we here?"

"Your witches called us Watchers. We received offerings. I recognized your girl from long ago. I was interested also to see you."

"Why me?"

"Daimones such as yourself are not unknown to fallen angels."

As a fallen angel, he outranked her. He could overpower and enslave her if she didn't have a protector.

"I work for Hekate."

"I know. And you go by Puabi-Ekur. Come, sit with me."

The angel turned and walked across the oasis. Puabi followed, curious and a little frightened.

A light breeze rustled the palm leaves. Across the sand ran a pavement of terracotta tiles. White lilies in pots bobbed gently as they skirted scattered low brown buildings. From somewhere flowed a current of jasmine scent.

Near the well, by a stand of palm trees, sat a bench, sand embedded in the whorls of its wood. Folding his wings away to another dimension, the angel sat, gesturing Puabi should follow. Wicked scars from long-ago battles crisscrossed his arm and hand, wreathing upward. A divot at the base of his thumb marked the entrance of some ancient blade.

"Would you like some wine?" A tray with a silver pitcher and two matching cups appeared between them, vines embossed on the silver. An odd offer—perhaps it had become ingrained for him when he was embodied.

"Not particularly. I'd like to know your intentions."

"Then I will be direct. I would like you to work for me. I have asked that your lady Hekate, Queen of the Angels, subcontract your services to me."

Could that be so?

"I need to talk to Hekate."

"Check with her now, if you so desire. I will wait."

The angel gestured, and a window opened—a simple rectangle cut into the air.

In black space, salted with stars, hung a throne flanked

by two torches in flame. On it, a goddess toyed with a key that dangled from a silver chain.

Was this Hekate? Spirits could be tricky. Azazel could be showing Puabi what she wanted to see.

As if in answer, garlic-smelling smoke rose.

Could he know about that? How far could he read her mind?

The lady tapped the key against her smile.

The goddess felt right to her. She trusted that.

"In answer to your question, Puabi-Ekur, yes. Azazel asked to work with you, and I am amenable. It is your choice."

"Will it help Joanie?"

"Perhaps."

Hekate was rarely forthcoming. There were many futures, constantly in creation and destruction. Yet she had never steered Puabi-Ekur wrong.

"Can I trust him?"

The goddess only smiled.

Hekate had agreed to let her do this work. Azazel must be trustworthy enough.

The window rolled up to nothingness and was gone.

"There are benefits to being in my service. Not least of all, my protection. I know in the past you fought the djinn. I can help."

Puabi-Ekur had vowed to stop drifting, to help Joanie and her people go forward. They also had responsibility to Gus, another lover from a past life.

That face as beautiful as a woman's, those eyes lined in black spoke too.

Before she'd loved Iltani, who was now Joanie, Puabi had

loved a prince. She'd never met a man better-looking than Azazel. He had the muscles to carry his armor, broad shoulders, powerful thighs, sinewed calves.

On the astral, you could present as you liked, though most spirits had signature forms.

While Puabi considered, a creature at least as old as she and more powerful was watching.

"Take your time to think. I can return."

"What does the work entail? How long is the term of service?"

"The work is specific to the job I have in mind, and ends with the success or failure thereof. At any time, you may call a meeting, refuse work, or end the contract and return to work directly for your goddess."

That seemed more than fair.

"But what is it?"

"It is a work personal to me, and I would want you under contract before I describe it. But rest assured that in no way would it be deleterious to your honor or karma."

It felt like a step in the right direction. She trusted Hekate.

"I'll do it."

"Very well then." Azazel stood, and Puabi followed. In these bodies, the angel was easily a foot taller.

Leaning down, Azazel kissed her on the forehead. "Welcome to my service."

Stepping back, he looked at Puabi, a hint of smile on his mouth.

"You could have more than a kiss on the forehead, if you like. To seal the deal."

This kind of line was Puabi's business. To be fed it in this situation was unnerving.

"As you desire. But even the book says it is what we Watchers came here for."

She was tempted to shift shape, to General Ekur. She suspected Azazel would change shape accordingly—to what, she didn't know. It might be interesting to discover. Like incubi-succubi, angels had a reputation for being gender-fluid. She doubted, though, that Azazel would bottom to her.

"Hold that thought," she said.

"Being what I am, I can hold it forever."

The pocket universe disappeared.

Chapter 4

*E*arly the next evening, cold lilac twilight filled the sky, which translated to a chilly room in the former garage. Joanie turned on her space heater.

It rattled, producing orange-red bars of heat. Joanie lit the coral-pink candle on her desk and began to meditate, letting herself drop back onto her quilt-covered bed.

After a few minutes, Puabi-Ekur appeared.

She bounced up. "Thank the goddess you're here. Last night—who was that in my space?"

"Azazel." Puabi-Ekur sketched their meeting.

"What's he poking around for?"

"The coven called the Watchers. More specifically, I don't know. But angels in general are messengers. They have other tasks—one is making war. As for the Watchers, you heard the Book of Enoch. They trained humans, perhaps before humans should have been trained, particularly in magic."

"Azazel brought cosmetics and war. Or metallurgy."

"Azazel also shows up later as the angel of sacrifice—you sacrifice the scapegoat to him in the desert."

"I still don't know if I like having angels in my witchcraft." Though the angels' story of being trapped in hell had moved her. She hated being trapped herself.

"Think of them as a form of spirit, a form with a particular focus."

"But angels serve the Judeo-Christian father-god. Jehovah. I mean, with all respect, I don't like Jehovah much."

Her mother remained Christian, and that meant Joanie had to distance herself. She had no time for patriarchal assumptions, something the Old Testament God was full of.

"I don't think the Watchers like Jehovah much either. Remember, they defied him to get with humans, and got damned for it. Legend has it Samyaza repented. Azazel is on record as not having done so."

"I like him better already."

"He said he knew you from before."

A trace of past-life memory fluttered by and faded.

"I guess how is obvious. He came down here to fuck, right?" She yawned and stretched. "At some point, we had sex. Which would explain him getting in my space like that."

He had audacity. She liked audacity.

"Even so, he can properly introduce himself. And pay the going rate."

Chapter 5

In the living room of Firebird House, full of bright-yellow sunflower paintings, the fifteen remaining members of Joanie's intentional community met. Till recently, there'd been twenty in the community. Now five lived in nearby apartments and ten in the house, including Joanie and Cleo. They gave each other chosen family and less expensive housing, supported a few folks who needed it, did Forum together to work out group issues.

Joe had made coffee, but it was evening, so only a few people filled cups in the kitchen. Joanie made herself peppermint tea and poured hot water for a few others. People draped themselves on the pair of oversized, chocolate-brown couches. A few grabbed straight-back chairs from the dining room, others folding chairs.

When everyone was seated, Cleo leaned forward in her chair, elbows on her knees. She'd dressed down, in black, her outfit's only color a lime-green headband holding back her short Afro. In the last few months, she'd taken on the role of working with the landlord.

"Everybody knows Emma died in late November, and her son Nelson has been showing the house." Emma had been their landlady, a child of the sixties and a fan of intentional community. "He sold it."

The group took a collective breath in.

"We get three months to find new housing."

Faces dropped across the room. Everyone had known it was coming; still it was a shock.

"It could be worse," Joe said, after a moment. Mid-forties, a software developer, Joe was a carpenter on the side. A few years ago a libertarian, he'd moved further left since then.

"After all, Nathan's a capitalist," Casey said under his breath. In his late fifties, he was an old-school anarchist.

Sherry rolled her eyes. "Yes, he's a capitalist. We were lucky to last as long as we did." Sherry was a veteran of a software union, now defunct.

"In Seattle?" Joe said. "This is a pretty liberal-left town. We should have tried to buy the house."

Before that argument started again, Cleo broke in. "There are other options, if we want a group house. We might be able to buy, if we found the right real-estate agent. When we met with the city, we learned Seattle is loosening the rules to permit the kind of housing we want."

She gave details. Joanie let her gaze skip across the room.

Maybe they could find a place together.

Did she even want that, at this point? Arguments had simmered over the last year that nothing had calmed. They'd exhausted her. Trying to buy or even rent together would only add more drama. They hadn't been able to agree to buy the current house; why would they agree on a new one?

"No need to decide right away, but we should make a move soon," Cleo said. "We can meet again and talk in a bit, if you all want."

"Should we order some pizza and talk now?" Joe asked.

"I need to think on my own," Casey said. With a grunt, he stood and left the room.

Sherry eyed his retreating back. "I'm in. I just need the cauliflower crust."

"Sure, sure," said Joe. "You're still gluten-free?"

She glared at him. "It really is helping."

"I think it's hype. But it's your body."

"It sure is, Joe."

Cleo glanced from one to the other. "Does anyone have any questions?"

Chapter 6

Over the previous year, Gus had maintained his friendship with Julia, whom he'd met through Odin's Hunt—formerly led by his white supremacist boyfriend, Max.

She'd left the Hunt also, driven out, harassed enough she had to move houses and drop off social media. She kept a friendship with Linda, the wife of Jake, another Hunt leader.

She and Gus met sometimes in the Beacon Hill coffee shop they'd frequented when it was near Julia's house, so she could let him know what the Hunt was up to. The front few rooms of a cottage, inside the café was simple, gleaming white, with open-format bookcases and small potted plants. When Gus arrived early to their meeting, he got his usual drip coffee.

Julia entered, her navy jacket beaded with rain. At the counter, she got a frappé, then sat across from him.

"How are you?" he asked.

"Fine. Tired. I'm starting to think I might have to renegotiate our joint custody. Noah's completely bored at his father's house. His dad just plops him in front of a screen and disappears."

"I'm sorry."

Putting his hand over hers, he stroked it. He wasn't a parent, but he'd argued with ridiculous exes.

"How about you?"

"Surviving." He was in his last year of college, finishing his last classes in biology. "I should be getting As. And I should be thinking about what to do next."

"Still planning to go into medicine?"

"Less and less. Or, at least, I don't want to be a doctor. I might go into nursing or EMT work or something. They both help people without requiring so much school. I don't think I can handle more school right now, or more school debt."

Julia downed a sip of her drink.

"You got whipped cream on your nose," Gus said. Reaching out a finger, he wiped it off.

She stuck out her tongue, and they grinned at each other.

It was always touch and go, whether they'd sleep together.

"Did Linda have anything to say about Max?"

"There was talk again at solstice that Max might come back from Europe, but that hasn't happened yet. I haven't heard anything since." Julia scooped up whipped cream with one finger and licked it off. "Here's hoping he stays there forever."

Chapter 7

$\mathcal{N}$ora's poison-path class met two Saturdays a month. Joanie got the time off, and Cleo decided to join her.

Classes started after Imbolc, the first of February. The challenge was finding a way out there. Nora lived in the woods, on the Seattle outskirts, an hour from the University District.

"I think it's time to get your car working or sell it."

It had been parked for more than a year on a side street. Joanie was surprised it hadn't gotten ticketed or stolen.

They walked to where it sat and wiped some wet dead leaves off it. Cleo frowned at it, arms folded. Behind her, on the sidewalk, Joanie paused to admire her.

She'd never gotten over that this beautiful, smart woman was her girlfriend. Today Cleo wore something only she could pull off, her hair left natural and tied up in a chartreuse-and-mustard sash, with a voluminous mustard-and-orange dress, over it a chartreuse duster, a multicolored wool scarf for warmth.

Joanie came up and wrapped herself around her, comforting herself with Cleo's sandalwood smell. Cleo glanced over her shoulder, patted her, and folded her arms around Joanie's.

"Do we know any car mechanics who might work cheaper than a shop?" Joanie asked. "Or for barter?" It was one of the things community was good for.

"Let's ask around. In the meantime, we could do some kind of hourly car rental. I'll split it with you."

A wet wind blew up, tossing Cleo's scarf.

"We need some good luck," she mused, gazing at the car.

"I'll call in some luck. We're witches, after all."

Cobalt blue flowed across the zenith, heralding the night. A bar of burnt-orange at the horizon struck color from the dunes.

A black tent splayed between the guy-lines that secured it. Within lay red-and-black-striped rugs and pillows. A silver tray held a matching pitcher and two cups, vines embossed on silver.

The bed sat low, its mattress on the floor. Thrown over it, a fur-lined coverlet lay with a corner turned down. The nights got cold.

In the dream, he came up behind her as she stood in the tent, putting his hands on her bare waist. Longing like a wave poured through her—nipples, pussy, mouth—herself gone liquid, melting at a touch.

He kissed then gently nipped her neck. A fragrance of dark frankincense rose, carried on the personal scent that was only his.

His low-pitched voice said, "What is your desire?"

At the sound, she woke. So strong was her sense of loss she started crying.

Chapter 8

breeze brought Puabi-Ekur the smell of dark frankincense.

This time, they met at the end of twilight, blue dark fading into night. Beyond the low brown buildings of the oasis, punctuated by golden-lit windows, a camp of black tents sat, fastened with pale ropes to stakes in the sand.

As before, Puabi-Ekur saw no one but him.

Azazel lounged on the bench by the palm trees, a silver wine cup in one hand. A breeze played around him, but he'd hidden his wings. The armor was also gone. He wore a long, simple robe, dark red, edged in dark-blue bands. Next to him on the bench sat the salver, pitcher, and another cup.

"Drink with me, Puabi-Ekur."

Again by instinct, Puabi-Ekur presented as female, as Puabi. But since Azazel had dropped warrior dress, she left off her silver-coin costume and wore a loose robe in black.

She let out a long breath, trying to calm herself. She'd know the task she'd agreed to soon.

"Yes, my lord."

He cut his eyes at her. "Please, no honorifics."

He poured her a cup of wine, and she sipped it, a dry red. Likely by the rules of the place it had the power of intoxication.

"I sent your girl Joanie a dream of me last night. She and I were married long ago."

Puabi-Ekur's protective urge leapt forward. "Please don't crowd her."

"She misses me. Women who were mine often miss me. You knew me then as well. Shall I tell the story? To begin at the beginning often helps."

A different desert, it had darker sand—he sent the image. Among its dunes sat a tent like the ones she'd seen past their meeting place, black, part of a small settlement, a long time ago.

"I traveled then with a loose group of followers, the pick of my Watcher comrades. With the goats, sheep, and donkeys, we moved between pastures."

He had come for the beauty of women; he had also loved men. In the city, he made silver jewelry, the pleasure of the rich, but for long periods he traveled in the desert and the highlands. With their herds, milk and cheese, leather and wool, his tribe was mostly self-sufficient, but he had a house in the city that a kinsman looked after.

It grew darker while he talked. Fires glimmered among the tents.

"As an alliance, for her beauty, and for love, I married

Saadiya. Then a rival clan murdered most of her family. Her grandfather saved her cousin, Zivah."

Here he looked up, light glittering on the whites of his eyes.

If the glance was supposed to tell Puabi something, she didn't know what. Nothing in his story so far had calmed her tension. Old feelings moved, below the cusp of consciousness.

"Zivah and her grandfather became part of my household."

Azazel poured himself another cup. By now, in the pocket universe, the stars had risen. The pitcher never emptied of wine. Puabi knew better than to drink quickly.

Light from a nearby building cast itself across the sand and gilded the side of the embossed wine pitcher.

"More?"

Puabi held out her cup. The sound of wine filling it echoed within.

The warm breeze tasted her skin. When it turned, she caught the scent of frankincense, mixed with something undefinable, his personal smell.

"Time passed. By my nature, I aged slowly. Saadiya's grandfather died, and it was past time for Zivah to marry. By then, I had known Zivah, and she was in love with me."

He looked into her eyes again. As if his gaze transferred the vision, she saw it.

The horizon of dunes pressed black against the paler evening sky. Stars glinted, faraway fires. Zivah was still a girl, a goatherd; it was time to call the animals in. She rounded them up with her staff to the half-musical, dissonant clank of goat bells, at last nudged the last goat into the paddock.

She turned toward the uneven hummocked tents, in the center of their arc a fire of acacia wood. As she came away from the paddock, Azazel strolled up.

"There you are. Come, food is prepared."

He was her cousin's husband. It was not unknown for a man to marry two cousins.

She stepped forward toward him as he did toward her. Not expecting it, he bumped into her. She caught his robe to keep him close.

"Zivah—"

She looked up, into his eyes, grey-blue, pale in this half-light.

Then she caught him behind his neck, pulled him toward her, and kissed him.

A sound of rushing filled her ears. A feeling of escape, of heat poured through Zivah like warm honey.

"I was Zivah," Puabi said.

Longing from the past welled up in her. It threatened her defenses, and she didn't want it.

"Your Joanie was Saadiya. Very like how she is now. I would recognize those black eyes anywhere."

"I pursued you?"

"You were in my power. If I wished happiness, it would have to be so." He smiled into his cup.

She wasn't sure what he meant. Had he groomed her?

"How was Saadiya with all this?"

"She wanted her cousin taken care of, and happy. We were equals in that marriage, as much as we could be in that time and place."

"She ran the household and your business."

"We ran them together."

"She had lovers?"

"She was discreet. We understood one another. We loved each other. That was often a violent, bitter world. For Zivah, if I could have found a better husband, I would have."

From Azazel, a dark wave of emotion swelled, passion undifferentiated. She couldn't make sense of it.

"We three lived together for years, till Saadiya died in childbirth."

"I was your wife?" The memory of a memory, it had a distant resonance, lust but also love and warmth.

"For fifty years."

"You loved both of us."

"Is that so hard to imagine?" Again he refilled for himself.

The scent of red wine floated to her. His breath sounded in his cup as he drank.

Puabi-Ekur took another mouthful.

Wherever he was leading her, she didn't want to go, not yet. Too much fear sparked, the fear of an animal of a cage. She didn't trust these old feelings.

She'd never considered how many lives she and Joanie might have spent together. This wandering life must have come after Uruk.

She had to focus. "I'm working for you. What do you want me to do?"

"What do you do well?"

"I am an incubus-succubus, as you know. I am dedicated to Inanna, I'm connected to Ereshkigal, and I work also for Hekate. For Hekate, it's mostly been about creating allies."

"You are persuasive, and you make connections. Before I make use of your skill, we need to get to know one another again. Learn each other's value. Now you have this story. It is a beginning."

Puabi-Ekur was themselves a seducer, had for centuries plied a particular trade. Coming in the night to those who lay dreaming or awake, to folk of all genders, they had persuaded the release of mind and body. They had taken seed and impregnated women. They had broken marriages; they had made marriages.

A seducer who listens, who supports, who would feed and protect you and your family, would take no for an answer not once but many times—is that seduction, or is that love?

Chapter 9

Once again, Firebird House met under the sunflower paintings. They had to decide whether to search for a house together or break the community up.

One core member was moving to Portland. Another was moving in with a partner, outside community. A handful wanted to rent together. Most did not.

Joanie sat in the corner, in a folding chair, watching, mostly not speaking. Cleo, central on one of the couches, voted that the largest group possible rent together.

But the few who wanted this weren't people who could live together. Joe, Sherry, Casey—if these three moved in with Cleo and Joanie, without the mediating influences of the people moving out, the house would always be at odds.

"Yeah, that's not going to work," Casey said. "I can't stand Joe without a lot of help."

"Back at ya," Joe said.

A hubbub broke out, everyone talking over each other.

Joanie caught Cleo's eye. Casey was right.

"We can still get together for Forum," Cleo said. "But for now, it's clear we should find separate rentals."

After the meeting, Joanie went upstairs with Cleo to her room. They threw themselves down, entwining on her bed, under her spangled sari. Cleo reached over and lit a candle, shining off gilt thread above and mirrors sewn on decorative pillows. She fell back and stared at the ceiling.

On her elbow above Cleo, Joanie stroked her cheek. "It's not what we wanted. But at least we figured it out now, not at the last minute. Firebird House isn't about the house—we can still be a community."

"There's not much chance you and I can find something decent in the U District."

"We could go north or south."

"I'm marginally more interested in north. It'd be easier to get to Nora's from there, as far as it goes."

"We'll find something." A small excitement burst—she'd be moving in with her girlfriend.

Candlelight glazed the room butter-yellow. The musky scent under sandalwood rose that was Cleo's own. No one kissed like Cleo: those sweet full lips, that orchid mouth, that tongue, tasting her neck. Pushing Joanie over, Cleo tugged off her t-shirt, licked and bit her nipples. Fingertips glancing across her skin. Under half-closed eyelids, Joanie saw Cleo watching her face. Joanie tried to hold her gaze, then shut her eyes.

A line, a cat-claw of almost-pain, drew along her skin, neck to feet—one of Cleo's toys, a spiked finger-covering. She wriggled, ticklish. Cleo's tongue followed with a liquid line.

In her hand she held a glass dildo, red and orange marbling on a white base, like a species of candy cane.

"You like cock? You like my cock."

"Yes," Joanie whispered.

The world flooded, broke to pieces, and reformed.

Full, taken, she basked in love like coming home.

In the morning, Cleo left for her office. Joanie had the day off, and accounting homework to do.

It was hard work, driving herself through it. When the ping from her email went off, she needed distraction.

It was more than distraction.

Your boyfriend killed Mark Walker because you told him to. You're not going to get away with it.

Chapter 10

$\mathcal{D}$ave, a security expert who had been a friend of Pete's, agreed to meet Joanie and Gus at Joanie's U District coffee shop.

Pale light of February fell from a sky smudged with cirrus. Alternating sun and shade flickered across the blonde wood table. She'd chosen a quiet time at the shop, midafternoon, and a corner booth. She nursed a cappuccino while she waited.

Dave came in and got a cold brew coffee. He worked in IT—tall, a bit heavyset, with a mane of dark hair and a short-trimmed beard.

He checked out the mail on her laptop. After a while, he pushed it back across the table, shaking his head.

"Like that email you got a year or so ago, it was sent through an anonymous proxy." The year-ago email had said almost exactly the same thing. They'd thought it was Max, but there was no way to be sure.

"No way to figure out where it comes from."

"No. I'm sorry I can't be more help on that."

Gus entered, grabbing some drip coffee came over to them. Typical of Gus, he wore all black—black t-shirt, black jeans. He'd dyed his hair again, the streak dark blue-green.

"Sorry I'm late." He glanced from one face to another. "The news isn't good?"

Joanie shook her head.

"Neither is mine. Julia let me know—Max has a plane ticket. He's going to go to his family on the East Coast. But after that, I bet he's coming here."

Dave grunted, "Shit." He covered his face with his propped hands.

Dave had connected to Pete through a loose group of Antifa and anarcho-communists. He'd known Rob too, another Antifa boy and another ex of Max's, whom Odin's Hunt had ritually killed. Now his anarchism focused on helping coordinate mutual aid, distributing free groceries in his neighborhood. Cleo and he had worked on some urban farming initiatives together.

"You both think this email comes from Max, don't you?"

"It feels like him," Gus said. "I mean, it's dumb, to telegraph your moves like that. But he likes to gloat. I guess he and Mark Walker were closer than we knew. Mark did tell Joanie they were friends."

Max had been Gus's boyfriend before he tried to kill Gus by throwing him off a mountain. The sex had been hot, and they'd shared a connection to the Norse gods, but Max's worship had turned out racist and violent.

A ray of sun crossed the blonde wood table, hid again.

"If Max shows up, Joanie, you are probably in danger," Dave said. "And Gus, you're definitely in danger."

"Maybe I should be worried, but I'm not," Gus said. "On the street, I stay pretty careful. At home, after we caught the Hunt breaking that window, we showed we'd take people to court. Bruni's on probation now. I know Max is all about his lawyer, but I don't think he'll take the risk."

Out the window, students passed, book bags sagging from their shoulders. A towheaded man leaned against the sign pole at the bus stop, folding a piece of pizza into his mouth.

"Plus, I don't claim to understand Max's way of thinking, but he puts stock in omens. I survived last time. Maybe that means he's had his chance at me. For now, I'd worry more about the explicit threat."

"What about you, Joanie?"

Under her surface numbness, as she held herself together, fear trembled.

"We don't know if it's Max for sure."

"True," said Dave. "A lot of stuff I'd think about for Max applies to the general case too, though. You're about to move, which is good. I would definitely only tell people your new location on a need-to-know basis. Try to stay in groups when you can. I know you started martial arts training with Pete. I'd pick it up again, if I were you."

Gus looked at her under his eyebrows.

"I have a martial arts background. I can help."

"I'll keep it in mind. But, since we're thinking it's Max, can we stop him before he's a problem? There must be something. He's been pretty violent."

"We can still try implicating him in Rob's death," Gus said. "My lawyer offered to suggest private detectives."

He blew on his still-hot coffee, took a sip.

"There's a few things in the way. Four people threw spears that night, and I don't know which one hit Rob. All four might be charged, which makes it less likely any one will step forward. Plus there's no body, and it was more than two years ago."

A group had settled at a table a few feet away. Dave glanced at them before speaking, and pitched his voice low.

"We know Max got rid of the body. Where would it be?"

"I'd guess he burned it or composted it, probably at Odinshof. There'd still be bones, though."

"You think we could find out where?" Joanie asked.

"Go through twenty acres of woods belonging to people who might kill us on sight, to find a burial more than two years old? Just besides having a huge area to comb, and not wanting to get murdered, none of us has that skill. I think we need a police forensics team."

"Can we get the law moving on it?"

"My lawyer nudged them a couple times. But Rob was an anarchist, not some cute little girl with pigtails. The police aren't interested."

"They should be."

"By and large, the police hate anarchists—you know that."

"Do we really have to let this go?"

Dave looked up. "I'm not going to let this go. But I don't think we can approach it from that angle. Or not just from that angle."

"If I can get some help with the money, I'm thinking now is a good time to ask my lawyer about private detectives. Maybe bring in this threat, Joanie, if you want that."

"But also—this smells like Max," Dave said. "I know him."

"I have to agree," Gus said.

"With some people it'd be an idle threat, to fuck with your head. But Max idolizes violence."

"There's something weird here, though," Gus said. "I agree, given the connection, something here says Max. But with Rob and me, it was personal. He felt betrayed both times. This isn't like that."

"Maybe Max needs to prove himself to some far-right group, here or in Austria," Joanie said. "Or maybe he and Mark were close, like you said."

"Mostly, we just need to stop whoever this is," Dave said. "Given what we're saying, if it's Max, we may need to be ready to catch him in the act."

Joanie swirled the remaining foam in her cup.

"It's too bad Firebird House is breaking up. One of the great things about community is there's always people around."

"There's Hannah and the coven. And Cleo. Cleo would defend you with her life."

Cleo, with Joanie's then-boyfriend Clayton, had thought up the plan that saved Joanie from her vicious sugar daddy. Clayton had finished his degree in California and signed on with an engineering firm there. He had a girlfriend—Joanie occasionally talked to him on the phone.

"Maybe whatever place we get, I should spend more time at Hannah's."

"Or at least with someone around."

Dave looked at his phone. "I have to take off. I can follow up with ideas about steps to take. I feel like I owe it to Pete to help his friends, and security is a particular interest of mine."

"I'd like that."

They all stood. Joanie hugged Dave good-bye.

The glass door of the shop hung on its spring, then closed behind him. She sat back down across from Gus.

"How do you feel about Max coming back?"

"Weird. Not good. I kind of shoved all that in a box and left it."

It was one thing they had in common—Joanie had nearly been killed by her sugar daddy, and Gus had nearly been killed by Max. She reached out and took his hand, squeezed it, let it go.

"I'd like to take you up on your offer about martial arts training."

Chapter 11

$\mathcal{A}$t Firebird House, when consulted about security cameras, people brought up privacy concerns—they didn't want their comings and goings recorded. Many had seen leftist groups infiltrated and didn't want to feed into that. After a long negotiation, the household agreed Joanie and Cleo could mount cameras and keep a week's worth of footage, to be wiped when they left.

Firebird House agreed to let Joanie use the driveway to park her car, so she wouldn't have to walk home from random parking on her way back from Nora's. Within the house, everyone agreed to stay alert to possible calls for help.

Her remaining safety exposure was her walk to work. There was no getting around that. She could walk faster than she could catch a bus, almost faster than she could drive, and it was ruinously expensive to park in the University District.

The advice was to vary her route. Which she would do, but with every path there were choke points, corners she'd end up on even if she took a wide loop into the university grounds.

Gus picked up Joanie's training under the Tree of Life hanging in the basement of the covenstead—Hannah's house in North Seattle, where he lived.

Repurposing sleeping mats, he threw several on the floor and held one up with both hands. "Show me some punches."

"Give me a second." Joanie shook out her hands, took a few deep breaths, then launched into it.

Thwack, thwack, thwack.

She'd gotten over her hesitation when she worked with Pete, and now used her full force.

"Pretty good. I can see you have some training. Did you do kicks?" She nodded. "Show me some of those."

She kicked, letting herself pour her body into it—a way to be present. She'd never imagined herself kicking ass, but she could kick ass. She'd been in pretty good shape even to begin with. Now again, she brought all her force to bear.

"Nice! Especially since you haven't been practicing."

He worked her till she was sweating and out of breath, and then they threw themselves down on the couch.

"My background is a mix of karate, kung fu, and a couple of street fighting styles. I think I can show you some things."

"That sounds good." She sipped water from a cup she'd carried down. "What's Max like, anyway?"

"Insane. He's a good fighter, too, and he keeps himself in shape. If I know him, though, he's going to underestimate you. He's not a huge fan of women in general. If you do end up against him, surprise is your best friend. Also running."

"I can run."

"I really don't expect him to show up till March at the earliest, based on what I heard."

"Any movement on the private detective?"

"I went with the cheapest one. I set an appointment. What he told me on the phone was that we'd start with basic research, including if possible locating persons of interest."

Chapter 12

At nightfall at the oasis, a yellow-gold band lay along the horizon, blue-grey clouds floating in it. Sand eddied along the tiled path forward.

It was reflex now to present as Puabi. She wore a simple robe, draped, dark blue, with a yellow-ochre wrap that collected the dying light.

She found the sandy bench where they'd sat before, by its stand of palms. Sitting, she pulled her sandaled feet under her robe, though she wasn't cold. The wind whispered in the leaves.

This was an earthly place, somehow bounded—solid but with hazy edges, entered by dream. She wasn't sure how it worked.

The angel appeared out of the horizon and strolled up to stand over her. He wore only a long, dark-red kilt, a sigil necklace gleaming on his bare chest. No wings, but it was as if the shadow of them hung behind him. A breeze trailed him. His grey-blue eyes shone pale against black kohl and dark skin.

She stood up, for courtesy's sake. It brought her a handsbreadth away from him, into the warmth surrounding his body.

Their long-ago kiss in darkness swam up from memory.

"It's Dudael."

"Pardon, my lord?"

He sat. "Please, as I say."

Right, no honorifics. She sat also.

"What is Dudael?"

"This place. A container. A hell, if you like. Where the Demiurge locked me after I defied him."

"You showed up for Joanie in earthly space."

"I am kept below heaven. If someone calls me, I may go."

"This doesn't seem very hellish."

A smile lifted the corner of his lip.

"It is written that I hang upside down in a chasm, in utter darkness, forever. I am freer than described. I may decorate."

He rolled his shoulders. The wing-shadow was gone.

Lamplight from a nearby mud-brick building fell across the sand. Beside them appeared the silver tray, wine pitcher, and cups. He poured them both wine.

"Tell me about your alliances."

"What would you like to know?"

"Who, what, when, where, why."

"All of them?" She had lived millennia.

"The current ones."

She took a sip of wine. "I drifted a long time, but I came to my current connections because of Clayton. He was overcome, begging for someone to take over his life."

"So you did."

"Just in the one way, my calling. I possessed him first when he and his friends hired Joanie."

"Saadiya."

"Yes. I discovered she'd been mine in the land of two rivers, in Uruk. I'd let her die there, by not trying hard enough. I was not going to do that again. So I remade my alliance to Inanna, though it had been a thousand years."

"Inanna is known to me."

How would an angel, incarnate for the pleasures of sex, connect with the goddess of sacred whores?

They'd been lovers.

"I see," Puabi said.

The air smelled of woodsmoke and dark frankincense.

"Inanna pointed me to her sister, Ereshkigal, Queen of the Great Below."

"She is known to me as well."

"The same way?"

He shook his head. "But you—?"

"I am a succubus." She had an on-again, off-again dalliance with the Queen of Hell. "Inanna and Ereshkigal called in the Annunaki and we defeated Joanie's enemy. Then I took up work with Hekate. She sent me to Gus, to protect him from his lover who wanted to kill him."

"Let me see."

Puabi showed him that memory. Thrown from a cliff, Gus lay among snow-drifted black boulders as she pled with him to live.

"You saved him."

"I kept him alive long enough for the medical people to come in their mechanical bird."

"It is an age of wonders. And then?"

"Now I see Joanie and her people inching toward a future, a farm, reclaiming some old things and bringing in new. There is a hillside belonging to a goddess they call Dea. I made alliance with her at Hekate's urging. After that, there came forth a god from Joanie's lover, a horned god."

"Let me see."

She showed him the path, through woods of cedar and fir, to the cabin where Hannah led a group in ritual to connect to their god-selves. Joanie's boyfriend Pete leaped up, crying, "I am the Horned God!" Months later, he fought Joanie's would-be rapist on a hotel balcony, till they fell to the street.

"He sacrificed himself. This brings us to my territory."

"In a way, yes."

"Your alliances, then—Hekate, Ereshkigal, Inanna, and this Dea. And the horned god?"

"I helped Joanie connect with him, so through Joanie."

Azazel glanced across the pocket hell. In the near distance, the low tents peaked, a set of small hills in black woven wool.

"I told you I had a project," he said.

Among the tents were lights—lanterns and a small fire. Like wisps of smoke, spirits crossed her vision on the near side of the flames.

"My project is freedom."

Chapter 13

*I*n the midafternoon of a February day, overcast but not raining, Joanie drove to Nora's house, Cleo riding shotgun. They'd picked up Alyssa, now in back half-asleep. Far outside town, near the National Forest, they took roads draped in cedar and fir. A turn, another, then they found the gravel road off which the land lay.

A long driveway snaked down to a hollow edged with fir and cedar trees. This forest always brought a twinge of memory, of Pete. Though she hadn't dreamed of Pete these last nights—not for nearly a month.

The gardens around the house were wintered in, piled with mulch. Lanterns, now dark, stood along the path from the house to the yurt, which crossed a bridge over a brook. Nora held classes in the yurt, which bordered a meadow, green still in wet late winter. A pond lay at the meadow's edge.

The class collected on throw pillows on the floor of the yurt, edging near the heater with its blue gas flame. Joanie,

Cleo, Alyssa, Olivia and two other folks from Nora's coven, and two strangers, sat facing Nora, a tall, hatchet-faced woman, her grey-streaked hair pinned in a loose bun on top of her head.

"We're going to start slow and easy because it sounds like most of you are beginners. Who's gotten a chance to start the reading?"

Olivia's and Cleo's hands went up—Cleo, after her master's, could consume books like a bonfire.

Joanie put hers up tentatively. "I've started, but just barely."

"Me too," Alyssa said. The others shook their heads.

"That's fine. As you probably saw, where we're starting is a couple books on nightshades. For me, those are one center of the poison path, which is also called veneficium—the study of poisonous plants that can also be used as medicines and divinatory aids. One important term to know is entheogen, which means anything you can intake to bring the gods into your vision."

Nods went around the circle.

"It's an important part to get to know the plants themselves. For me, they're herbal allies, who work with us witches for mutual benefit. Let's start by meeting one of them." She stood, and the class followed. "Everyone, grab a pillow and bring it."

They followed her over the bridge and down a short, graveled path to a greenhouse, glass gleaming in fogged light. She led them to the back, to a set of shrubby dark-green-leaved plants covered with creamy trumpet-shaped flowers, most now shut. A few sat open, watching them.

"Datura. They bloom at night—moonflowers."

Alyssa's eyes were shining. She whispered to Joanie, "They make me think of Moonshadow. They're going to love them." Moonshadow was the spirit she'd been working with.

"Datura is highly poisonous, and I keep them enclosed to protect local wildlife. In small doses, datura is one of the ingredients of traditional witches' flying ointments. Which were probably not applied by broomstick to the mucous membranes, despite what you might have heard. Go ahead and sniff one of the open blooms—they're safe for that."

Joanie nosed into one, to a heavy sweetness like honeysuckle. She had no sense of poison.

"Find a spot with your pillow, and I'm going to lead you in a meditation to meet the datura spirit. I will create a container to make sure you're safe. She is an ally, but a powerful one, not to be treated lightly."

Nora led them into trance, giving them a space to meet datura. Even before she shut her eyes, Joanie got a flash of a beautiful woman in a cream-colored dress, by moonlight, beckoning her.

"Do you want me to meet you at work?" Cleo asked. She took her guard duties seriously.

"Sure, if you want," Joanie said. "You know I'm closing."

"I want to get a draft of this grant written. I'll probably show up toward the end of your shift."

"That works."

The coffee shop didn't stay open late, but an evening crowd came in for soup and sandwiches. The late shift ended at eight, and it would take a half-hour to close after that.

It was a quiet evening. After doing a cleanup pass, Joanie perched behind the counter on a stool and pulled out her laptop and accounting homework.

She was finishing a second bachelor's. Accounting was something useful she could do to have cash in her pocket. It gave her a second gig as needed, to work around the coffee shop. Maybe at some point she'd go out on her own.

She had an economics degree, and last year she'd had a promising start in the financial industry. She still stayed in touch with Monica from her former job at the planning firm. Now Monica was with another, larger firm, though restless herself.

At her former firm, Joanie's boss had insisted she help manage a questionable plan for Walker Nelson Hospitality, whose CEO, Mark, had decided to pursue her and had fallen off the balcony fighting Pete. In the aftermath, the financial firm disintegrated, and she'd come back to the coffee shop. The owner had hinted she might be able to move to general manager.

Perhaps over time she'd end up with the shop. Jeremy didn't want to run it forever. She loved coffee, though she wasn't the full-on aficionado Jeremy was. Coffee was another plant spirit with a devoted following, though not something to farm in the Northwest.

Only a few people came in that night—a woman who ate a cupcake and read a paperback, and a couple doing home-work themselves, having finished their sandwiches.

Cold February wind shook the panes of the shop's

picture windows. Though it was only seven-thirty, midweek the University District streets were quiet.

Despite coffee, she was having a hard time focusing.

She cast her glance at the dark window, dreamily.

Pete popped into her mind, close-cropped red hair, slim and muscular body. His apotheosis as the Horned God had left her missing him, but also with a friend on the astral.

His demeanor was tense, his muscles tight, his face in a frown.

The lone woman pushed her way out the door, and a man came in. Muscular, shaved-headed, tattooed, he wore a white t-shirt and black hoodie. He read as a gay muscle daddy. "Double espresso, please."

He paid, waited as she pulled it; she handed it to him and went back to her laptop. He took a booth and started scrolling on his phone.

The couple showed themselves out. "Have a nice evening!" she called to their departing backs. The glass door hung on its spring then closed behind them.

Chapter 14

"Freedom?"

For a pocket hell, Dudael seemed comfortable, even if it never saw the midday sun. It cycled from twilight to night, back to dawn—she had never seen the whole process.

"Not for myself. I have my path and my agreements. For my people."

He gestured to the black tents, silhouetted against the night sky, and the shadowy forms by the fire.

"My angel legions followed me into exile. They have stayed with me for millennia. It is past time for many of them to take the next steps in their journey."

She looked closer. Among the tents gathered a company of soldiers, some in Mesopotamian fish-scale armor. When she looked, most had wings.

"How do you make that happen?"

"There are prayers and workings for the ascension for human souls, offered by humans. There are the same for angels. But my legions are trapped, without recourse to these."

The lantern light that poured across the sand only got as far as the foot of the bench. The sand reflected light upward. The golden half-light illumined his face, beautiful as a statue's, its planes and angles as clean as if cut from stone. His eyes were in darkness.

"How do you know this?"

"It has been known for millennia. Watcher angels—" he looked away, gave a short exasperated laugh. "We are notorious. We are in stories, legends, those illuminated games."

She stared. "You mean video games?"

"Yes. Most merely greet us or ask for things, or try to draw us into some—" he shook his head, closing his eyes— "sticky machinations, some imagined story. But over millennia, some have wished to help my people. Their prayers and workings failed."

"Why?"

"I have a theory. I might have a way to circumnavigate this. But for this working I need human help."

His gaze lay on her. She sipped her wine.

"It must be of a particular kind. To find and do the rituals requires at least suspension of disbelief. To be effective requires dedication. Of the few who might entertain the possibility, many consider it heresy or sin. Others consider the concept unpalatable."

"So Joanie and me are something of a find."

"One might think my former wives somewhat inclined to help me."

He gave her a look under his brows. She glanced down.

"You come on pretty strong."

"For angels, to speak is to do. That does not excuse my actions, however, if you felt attacked."

Angels were messengers, warriors, made of fire, living in the eternal present.

"Not attacked, but you take getting used to."

His eyes glittered as they moved. "This is my most human form."

He radiated impatience—no, he radiated anger and pain, but he reined himself in hard. She almost reached across and patted his wrist, but she didn't. He seemed as safe to touch as fire.

Chapter 15

The wind rattled the shop's plate-glass windows, black against night. A movement in the corner of her eye made her start, but it was nothing, a flash of light off the glass.

She glanced up at the remaining customer, his strong shoulders hunched in his black hoodie. He was studying his phone.

She'd been in the shop so often alone or nearly alone, and up until recently had always felt safe. The email threats had put her on edge.

She went back to her accounting homework. You could give a debtor a discount for prompt payment. Provision for bad and doubtful debts was deducted from the debtor total.

The sound of the wind shaking the panes distracted her. A splash of coffee on the counter needed wiping up.

The guy was still on his phone. Something about him bothered her.

Maybe she needed more coffee to focus. She locked her laptop and slid off her stool.

The gaze of the man in the hoodie fell on her. It felt hot, almost hateful.

She'd never asked Gus what Max looked like.

She gave the guy a quick grin as she would any customer, and slid out of view behind the coffee machine.

They'd made sure she was protected for Firebird House and her walk to work. They'd never considered an attack at the coffee shop. Mostly it was full of people, but not at the end of an evening shift.

She inched back around the machine. The customer had stood from his table. She stared, immobilized, deer in the headlights.

Putting his phone in his back pocket, he walked toward her. He took long strides, as if in slow motion.

Fuck being polite.

She grabbed her phone and ran.

Out through the back, the slippery floor just mopped—she slid and righted herself. She raced through the tiny storeroom, dark and full of boxes.

A thump, boots hitting the floor—he'd vaulted the counter.

She tugged at a standing shelf, hoping to pull it down. It didn't budge.

Footsteps pounded, closing on her.

She slammed out the back door into the alley.

Spinning in muck, she grabbed a dumpster to stop her slide, aimed toward the closest major street, University Avenue. She dodged garbage, sidestepped a sludge of leaves and a random milkcrate, flew through the alley.

She paused at the mouth. Odd even on a weeknight, the Ave was a ghost town—grey sky, low clouds, gusts of wet wind. Which way to run?

Footsteps pummeled closer.

She turned to run. But she'd taken too long to choose. He grabbed her from behind and dragged her backward.

The cold edge of a blade pressed her throat.

She dropped with all her weight. He held on.

No way to call Cleo.

Puabi-Ekur!

Chapter 16

In the shadow of the palm trees, Puabi leapt to her feet.

"She's in trouble. I have to go."

Standing, Azazel reached out a muscled arm. In his hand appeared a sword, glinting in fallen lamplight, a knuckle-sized red stone in the pommel.

"I promised to protect you. I want to protect Saadiya. May I fight by your side?"

"Sure! But we've got to go!"

He sheathed the weapon in its shoulder harness—he was now wearing armor. "Take my hand." His wings flared.

Then they were in the alley, behind Joanie, who was thrashing, held from behind by a man shaven bald, all muscles.

Puabi recognized him.

Max.

Azazel strode forward with his sword.

To fight, Puabi-Ekur changed shape to Ekur. He pulled his sword and fell into step by instinct.

In the world, the two appeared as wind. A knife-edged gust spun up, hit Max, and shoved him backward. Joanie twisted out of his grasp and ran, to the main street and down it.

Max stumbled to his feet, throwing himself forward. Azazel as a black wind knocked a wooden pallet off a dumpster in front of him. He tripped and fell. Azazel threw most of another pallet on his head, hard, and knocked him out.

Another section of pallet lifted off the dumpster.

"Don't kill him," Puabi said, returning to her female shape.

Their eyes met.

Black wings enveloped her, and they were gone.

Through the windy grey night, Joanie ran a block to a brew pub, stopped inside the red-painted alcove by the door.

The bouncer gave her a glance. "ID."

"I work up the street, at the coffee shop. A guy just came in and attacked me, chased me out. Okay if I stand here a moment?"

"Sure. But show me your ID, just in case."

"It's up at the shop."

The bouncer shrugged. "Just don't go inside."

Slipping her phone out of her back pocket, she dialed Cleo.

After a few phone calls, Jeremy agreed to come close the shop. Cleo walked Joanie home.

In February darkness, bare-branched trees shook their arms at the sky. A twisting wind blew through them, but only the usual kind. Back in the alleyway, the wind that had blasted Max had been something else.

She had called, and Puabi-Ekur had saved her.

"I can't believe we didn't cover the coffee shop," Cleo said.

"What we did worked."

"Because of good luck."

Joanie squeezed Cleo's hand.

"More like spirit protection."

Next day, they held a war council by video call: Cleo, Alyssa, Dave, Gus, and Joanie. Joanie and Cleo huddled in Cleo's room, under the spangled sari. Alyssa and Gus called from their tiny shared room at Hannah's.

"Should we just make sure you're always with another person when you're not home?" Alyssa asked.

"I need to step up my conversation with the private detective," Gus said.

"This was a success," Dave said. "Joanie didn't get beaten up or killed. Max showed his hand and didn't get what he wanted. It was scary, a near thing, but a success."

"I just don't want it to happen again," Joanie said. Part of her was still freaking out.

"Obviously. Doing what you did made it less likely to happen again. We found a chink in our armor, and we need to fill it. We have to make sure Joanie isn't alone at the shop."

"Did the cameras there catch him?" Gus asked.

"Probably, but he jumped me in the alley."

"From an anarchist point of view, we shouldn't support the police state," Dave said. "We know what's going on; we know who Max is. Camera footage would be to show the police."

Gus grimaced. "I'm not going to play the classical anarchist here. Getting the police involved when Bruni attacked the house hit Odin's Hunt hard, which was good."

"For me," said Joanie, "I want him caught and out of my life, and not endangering anyone else. Letting Max stay free is supporting fascism."

The meeting broke up. Over email, they arranged shifts to be with Joanie at the shop, the rare times she closed alone. Jeremy, the shop owner, pitched in to make sure she was on two-person shifts as much as possible.

Chapter 17

*I*n Dudael, after midnight, stars flared big as watchfires. Constellations wheeled above, spangled Orion at zenith. Perhaps Samyaza hung there.

"I'm in your debt," Puabi said.

Azazel threw himself back onto the wooden bench, lifting his long hair off the back of his neck with one hand, as if sweating. A light breeze circled him, ruffling the palm leaves. His armor and wings were gone; he wore a loose robe, in the dark shade of red he favored. Puabi had donned her black robe.

"Being in debt isn't a comfortable place for me."

His eyes glittered.

"Do you need reassurance?"

"What task do you require of me, exactly?"

"I need to free my legions. I need a pathway. I have seen a pathway through and a pathway around. You know the Lion-Faced, the Fool?" She stared. "Yaldabaoth. The Demiurge."

She knew whom he meant: the chief archon, god of the

manifest world, who'd tried to deny humans knowledge. Many confused him with the highest deity. He pretended to that throne. Or so some said.

"I avoid philosophy."

He leapt to his feet.

"This is not philosophy! He is the one who exiled us—who imprisoned us, after we came to Earth to teach and make love. Let him have his fight with me, but I will not let him trap my people. We have tried to propitiate him. It did not succeed. We must work around him."

"Sure."

"Puabi-Ekur, I have work to do here. I have asked your service. Are you with me?"

He stared at her.

"What? I'm just—"

"You are dragging your feet, succubus." His hands fisted at his sides. "Are you with me?"

Tall, with his long black mane all curls, eyes shining, muscled arms, the flicker of wings not quite there—in all, he was frightening.

"I don't want to fail you or Hekate."

"I need more than that. I need to succeed."

She stared up at him from the bench.

His blue-grey eyes glittered like jewels, blue topaz. His anger was like fire.

But it was aimed at their mutual enemy. She had sworn to engage more with life. Hekate had given her someone who'd drag her in kicking and screaming.

"Yes. I am with you."

He threw himself down again.

"Very well."

The wine once more appeared.

"Let us toast our endeavor. Because we will conquer."

The cups clanked together. She sipped, red wine on her lips, fear tight in her stomach.

To commit was to have something to lose.

Bit by bit, incarnations had taken things from her, had taken people from her. Joanie as Iltani. Sarah, burned as a witch. Maghavatii, likewise burned alive. That had been her last incarnation as a human.

"We need to take the pathway around Yaldabaoth. Before he declared himself king of heaven and earth, others ruled."

He caught her gaze.

"My ladies." Inanna, Queen of Heaven. Ereshkigal, Queen of the Great Below.

"Just so. I look particularly below, because of old it was given to the chthonic deities to release humans. But spirits cannot ask for release themselves. Humans must ask for redemption, even for angels."

"Is that so?"

"The rules may change at the whim of the Demiurge. But request is the most direct route."

He had come to her because she had all the tools within reach.

"You believe if Joanie asks Lady Ereshkigal for the release of your company, it can happen."

He shrugged. Again behind his shoulders she saw the great wings.

"Nothing is certain. But that is my thought. Some say angels cannot be redeemed, but I have seen some forgiven— and some change sides."

"I'll do it. I'll do my best to get my ladies and Joanie to help. I have a boon to ask in return."

A dark wing twitched.

"Anything within my power that is not harmful."

"I'll ask Joanie to ask for my freedom too."

Closing his eyes, he tipped his head back, showing his vulnerable throat.

"Your release is not in my hands. Your queen is Hekate. By all means ask. Now, if you like."

Sitting up, with one finger he drew a rectangle in the air, a window deep black against the translucent sky. It showed a throne in space, flanked by two torches aflame.

The throne was empty.

"Deities are fickle. Burn incense. Throw yourself at her feet."

Before them appeared a brazier. He tossed toward it a handful of herbs.

"Cypress, mint, storax, myrrh, willow, aconite."

On the coals, they burst into flame and sweet poisonous smoke that hinted of pine and mint.

She prostrated herself before the flames.

When she looked up, Azazel was gone.

Chapter 18

On her way to Gus's for martial art practice, Joanie jumped off the bus partway there to walk.

They'd gotten a warm spell mid-February. Wind tossed the bare branches; torn-edged clouds sailed across blue. In Hannah's yard, south facing, a few early crocuses bloomed at the base of an ancient maple: red-purple, open-mouthed, yellow-orange stamens. She knelt by them, breathing in their fragrance, the scent of spring and hope.

She was early; she hoped to catch Hannah, who worked from home.

She knocked and rang. Since the attacks last year, the household kept the door locked.

Hannah trundled up. "Joanie! What a pleasant surprise! I don't think Gus is home yet, but you're more than welcome to wait."

"I was hoping to talk to you, if you've got a minute."

"I was just putting on the kettle for some tea."

She followed Hannah back through the long, narrow

railroad kitchen, squeezed into a chair in the tiny dining room, bright with a red-and-white checkered tablecloth.

"I wanted to ask you—sometimes I have dreams of Pete."

"Oh, honey." Hannah sat down, putting her hand over Joanie's.

Joanie closed her eyes a moment to let the grief pass.

"Thanks. They've backed off, the last bit. But when I try to reach him in meditation, I almost always can't."

The kettle whistled.

"I'm making a pot of chai—want some?"

Hannah poured the boiling water over the tea ball and put the pot on a trivet to steep. Clove and cinnamon drifted in the air, woven with the tannin scent of tea.

"It's been a bit more than a year since he died. In the traditions I've studied, you try not to bother the dead for the first two or three years."

"Does that still hold for a demigod? Or whatever Pete became?"

"I don't know, but if you can't reach him, that process might be why. I suspect if you really need him and call him, he'll come."

She poured out a cup of tea for Joanie in one of the pretty cups she collected. This was pink with gold trim, with a spiderwebbed brown crack.

"You take milk?"

Joanie nodded. "Speaking of calling folks—the other evening, when Max jumped me, I called Puabi-Ekur. They weren't the only one who showed up."

She took a mouthful of tea.

"A big wind came up, and a pallet lifted off a dumpster and fell on Max. I told you I had that brief spirit visitation, at the Watchers ritual? I feel like it was him. Whoever that was."

"One of the Watchers, I'd think. They're also the Witch-fathers. Here to look after witches."

"I had a dream about him, like we were lovers. Not really a sex dream, though we kissed."

Hannah grinned. "Nice work if you can get it."

"I think I know him from a past life, if that could be. I think he's trying to get ahold of me."

"Do you want to him to?"

"I'm not sure. He really got in my space the first time. But in the dream I was longing for him."

"I'd try to be certain what I wanted before I called a spirit in, especially one as intense as a Watcher angel. Though people call them to guard the quarters. The lore says they're our ancestors, on our side—that's why they're called the Witch-fathers."

The front door opened to Gus. Tossing his daypack aside, he crossed into the kitchen and sat next to Joanie at the table.

"You're early! I'm just getting back from class."

"Want some tea?" Hannah asked.

"Sure, if you've got extra. I wanted to tell you both, I saw the private detective yesterday."

"Oh yeah?" Hannah said.

"He checked into what happened to the guys who were part of the ritual where Rob was killed. Of the guys besides Bruni and Max, one moved to Portland. Another left Odin's Hunt and is keeping his head down. There was also some background on Max's time in Austria."

Hannah poured tea.

"Is it hard to talk about? We don't have to."

"It's not that. It's just—I don't know if Max was always this person. But it's not who I remember."

A ray of sun glanced across the table.

"So the Freedom Party is the far-right Austrian political party Mark Walker's wife was associated with. Some of them have contact with groups that keep themselves under the radar. A sort of loose consortium, Austrian but also German, connections in the Slavic countries, all the way up through Scandinavia. White power, black metal. Max jumped right in. In a way that's always been his thing, but these folks are connected with the black metal church burners, what's left of them. I thought he aimed higher than that. He used to be all about the numinous, the level beyond this one."

"You can be an occultist and still be a shitty person," Joanie said.

"Interpol ties them to a string of murders—take that for what it's worth. It could indicate how Max moved to more general violence, from only attacking his exes. Also, we knew that Mark knew Max. Maybe they knew each other better than we realized. Enough that Max wants vengeance."

"Monica told me Mark had some dirty dealings," Joanie said. "Who knows, maybe he was supporting Odin's Hunt somehow, before all this? I could see him using them as thugs. What's next?"

"The detective offered to talk to the Hunt guys who left— he thinks that's our strongest lead. But I said to hold off."

"Why?" Hannah asked.

"I've spent all our money, and it'd be another chunk to do more work."

"Pretty sure we can raise it."

"Also, it'd mean poking the bear. The more nervous the Hunt is, the more likely they are to do something stupid. It's bad enough Max is in town, but so far it seems like he's acting alone."

He stood.

"Ready to kick and punch things?" he asked Joanie. "We can try some floor work, too, if you want."

"Whatever you think, Sensei."

"Don't call me that."

Wednesday night, an email appeared in her inbox:

> Your boyfriend killed Mark Walker. You're going
> to pay.

Thursday night, she got this:

> You think you're going to escape the wrath of the
> gods?

Friday night:

> Wounded to death, have I seen a man
> by the words of an evil woman;
> a lying tongue had bereft him of life,
> and all without reason of right.

"That's a verse from the Elder Edda," Gus said.

"Yeah, I looked it up."

Joanie was over at Hannah's, downstairs in the basement sorting the herb cabinet, which took up most of an alcove. She'd added tags and labels on jars that didn't have them and rewritten smudged ones: bay leaves dedicated to Helios; mint belonging to Hekate; powdered mugwort for prophetic dreams. Sheaves of lavender and rosemary hung drying from hooks above the cupboard, releasing scent when touched. She'd pulled out her laptop and showed the mail to Gus.

"Maybe he's getting frustrated? That might be good, force his hand."

"I'm tempted to do a no-contact order."

"We don't have much proof yet. When he jumped you, only you saw him."

Joanie glared at him.

"We'll get proof," he said. "On a brighter note, you're getting pretty good at your punches."

Good enough to fight Max? She doubted it, with his arms like steel girders, and fast on his feet besides. But it might give her the element of surprise. And they'd stepped up protection.

She called up the stairs to Hannah: "I've got this bunch jarred and labeled. You want it shelved in alphabetical order?"

"That'd be great. Is Nora planning to have y'all make flying ointment?"

"Not for several classes."

"Damn, I was hopin' we could use it for Imbolc." They'd pushed out the celebration of the Sabbat waiting for a couple out-of-towners to return.

"I'll ask if she has any."

Hannah stumped downstairs.

"It might be a great way to go visit your boyfriend. Or your new boyfriend?"

Joanie raised an eyebrow.

"Angel boyfriend," Hannah clarified.

"I'm not sure I want an angel in my witchcraft, let alone my bed."

"At least he's a fallen angel."

On the floor, among the jars of herbs that waited to be labeled, Gus perked up.

"I don't know about you, but I'd totally be down for Fallen Angel Boyfriend."

"If he helped protect you from Max, maybe do him a solid," Hannah said.

"Hmm. It is worth something to keep Max away from me."

Chapter 19

The basement of the covenstead lay with its alcoves in shadow. Magical incense burned. Coveners stood in a circle in front of the Tree of Life hanging, each wearing something pajamalike, loose black or red gowns, pants, t-shirts.

Facing the altar, Hannah called the goddess of the rite.

"I call Lady Brigid, lady of Imbolc, healer, herbalist, seer. This night, in dreams or visions, give each of us answers to our questions."

She turned back to her coven.

"Find a comfortable place to lie down and roll out your sleeping bag." They were all prepared to spend the night, though some would leave the ritual room to sleep separately.

Joanie set up near Cleo. Reaching out, she squeezed her girlfriend's hand, then lay looking at the ceiling painted with candlelight.

They passed around the tin of flying ointment. Around it hovered a scent of datura, almost like peanut butter, mixed with the green of other witch-herbs. They anointed their armpits and the creases of their thighs.

"If you haven't tried this before, be conservative. Recommended first dosage is a pea's worth under each armpit. I use more, but I'm a big girl with a hard head."

In meditation, Hannah guided them down a flight of steps. For Joanie, the steps paved themselves in black marble, and the lamps were gilt candelabra. A door at the bottom of the steps opened to visioning space.

For her, it opened to desert.

Dunes reared knife-cut against a dark-blue sky, the trees of an oasis nearer than the dunes. Tents ranged on the outskirts of the trees; closer in stood buildings, windows lamp-lit.

Footsteps sounded, scratching against sand.

A silhouette appeared, black against blue, then came into form, chiaroscuro in falling lamplight.

He wore a long dark-red kilt but was naked from the waist up, a gold sigil necklace dangling on his muscled chest. Broad-shouldered, brown-skinned, he wore his curling black hair unbound. His shadowed eyes, lined with kohl, glimmered pale grey-blue.

She hadn't remembered his beauty.

"Greetings, most fair."

"Greetings. I owe you thanks."

The corner of his lip turned up in a smile.

"I missed you too, my lady."

The memory of the dream poured through her. She flushed. Longing rose in a wave. It curled around him, rousing some long-ago feeling, love and lust and a deep trust beyond words.

He stepped close to her, eyes questioning; she nodded.

His arms came around her; he was so much taller she stood on tiptoes. She leaned in.

His lips soft, his scent surrounded her, dark frankincense. He kissed her, his seeking tongue tangled with hers, drawing up the wave of longing.

She had forgotten this.

Tears rolled down her face.

"It's been so long."

In that visionary space, dipping along points of a time-line, she saw the life in the desert. She saw like beads on a string a later life in a city near that desert and an encounter in a medieval European town. A bedroom, whitewashed plaster, the wooden frame of a bed—fleeting images passed. But what she wanted was here.

"There is no hurry, but neither need we wait. Come with me."

Taking her hand by two fingers, he led her along a sandy path past the tents, a path lined with torches.

In waving light and shadow, dark against darkness, a magnificent pavilion stood, black silk. He drew back the curtain of door. The tent stood two stories tall, lit within by gilt candelabra with only just enough candles. A bed dominated the space, dressed also in black silk, with a gilt headboard and frame.

"Wine?" He gestured to a pitcher on a low table.

"What I want is you."

Azazel grinned.

"You were ever thus."

"Skip to the good stuff, I say."

"Slow down, fire of my heart. It has been a few centuries. I want to greet you properly."

She opened her mouth to protest, but he laid one finger on her lips.

"Ssh."

Still standing, he picked up the fall of her dark hair, stroking her nape so she shivered. He kissed her neck, her collarbones, her cleavage. His hands cupped her breasts, pinching her nipples.

She threw her head back. He kissed along her neck, his hands skimming her back, her ass, teasing.

"You were always—"

"A tease? I deliver what I promise. I believe you move too quickly."

Slipping away, she threw herself onto the bed and pulled down its coverlet. She tugged her long black gown over her head, snagged and yanked off her underwear. She leaned back, naked and pale against his black sheets.

"I would have taken those off kiss by kiss."

"I know!" She waved him forward. "I want you now!"

He suppressed a laugh.

"No."

He climbed onto the bed, still in his kilt, sat back, kneeling on his heels. Sitting up, she lunged at him, kissing him; he caught her face, with both hands held her behind her jaw, kissed her deeply.

Probing and questing with their tongues, they relearned each other. Her tears fell into her mouth, a slight taste of salt.

Sitting back, he took her legs in both hands and pulled her forward, sliding her along the sheets, and spread her thighs. Sliding between them, he drew a finger down her stomach, across her pubic mound, to the flower of her vulva. Stroking her with his fingers, he watched her face.

"Sweetness, what do you like best, if I touch you, if I taste you?"

"I like it all! I want to fuck!"

"Not yet."

He moved his fingers.

"Too intense. No—there."

Hands cupping her thighs, he applied his mouth, reaching up now and then to tease her nipples.

Golden light lapped the height of the tent; the wave of pleasure went higher and higher, till she cried out.

He sat up smiling, face glistening.

She drew him forward and kissed him, tasting herself.

"Please fuck me."

"So impatient."

Her hand found the edge of his kilt, slipped under, and grasped his cock. He closed his eyes. With the other hand she scrabbled at the fastening, undid the kilt, and tossed it aside.

"Please."

He shackled her wrists to the bed with his hands, kissed her once more. Placing himself, he shoved inside her.

She moaned.

Watching her face—he knew her well, she hadn't changed—her eyelids fluttering, yes, yes, yes, there—

He released himself right after she climaxed, a splash of fire into the night.

～

After a short sleep, Joanie woke, deep in the night, in Hannah's basement.

It ripped across her heart. On some level, she had expected to wake in his arms—start over again, better, getting to know him again, reconnecting with the deep past he'd shown her, when they were married.

She heard him laughing, far away.

Who had paid whom back? This gift had gone both directions.

They hadn't had a chance to talk.

The next time she awoke, Cleo was stirring next to her. Rolling toward her, Cleo kissed her on the cheek: orchid lips, and the scent of sandalwood.

"Hi, sweetheart," Joanie said. "What did you get for a vision?"

"I visited my mighty dead, my ancestors in Africa. I got their blessing. And you? Did you meet your angel boy? You were squeaking."

"Was I loud?"

"No." Cleo traced a finger down her cheek. "I just know you pretty well."

"Good. I did see him. We had sex. I don't know if it counts as payback, though." She told the story.

"That sounds more like mutual appreciation."

Hannah got them all up to end the ritual. Scruffy, bed-headed, mussed with sleep, they opened the circle.

"Some of your visions will be the beginning of further exploration. You can reach this place again, likely with ordinary deep meditation. The flying ointment is made of entheogens, but they just make the travel easier."

She could get back to Angel Boyfriend—start learning him again. In other meditations, she had seen her past in Uruk with Puabi-Ekur. What had her past been with the angel? She'd only seen those few hints.

For all he read her like a book, there'd been very few beads on that thread. If he came back now, likely he had a reason to.

Chapter 20

ixing Joanie's car gave her and Cleo more range in apartment hunting, though Cleo still needed bus access. They'd found a few options, none they liked.

They'd checked in with Hannah, but she expected no openings at her house soon. They could couch-surf there indefinitely, but they needed a permanent home.

Now it was March, and they only had a month left before they were homeless.

Sitting in Cleo's bedroom, under her spangled sari, they hunted online—Craigslist, apartment sites.

"I want to stay north. I want easy access to the covenstead and Nora's. Forty-five minutes' drive beats a full hour."

"I wish Hannah had openings."

"But she doesn't." No rooms would open till September at the earliest—too long to wait.

"Ideally I'm still wanting a two-bedroom."

"We'll know it when we find it."

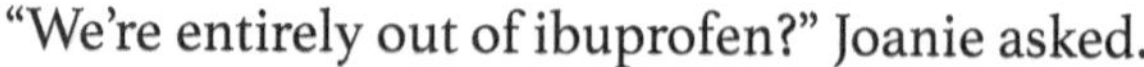

"We're entirely out of ibuprofen?" Joanie asked.

"I guess so. I'm kind of surprised," Casey said.

One of her least favorite people at the house, Casey agreed with her philosophically, in general. But he was in his late fifties, ponderous and sententious.

Now he was lounging on the couch, reading a tech book to brush up on Python programming.

Her period was coming on. She needed ibuprofen now, would only need it more later.

To drive to the drugstore was stupid. It was walking distance. With parking, it would take her more time to drive than walk.

She went to the coat closet, found and pulled on her jeans jacket.

He looked at her over his reading glasses. "You going out? Aren't you supposed to always have protection against your stalker?"

His tone sounded parental, as if she were being a bad child. Offering to walk her wasn't Casey's style.

The whole thing annoyed her, feeling trapped in the house like a child or pet. Or she might have waited and asked Cleo to pick up ibuprofen on the way home, or asked around for a roommate's stash.

Fuck it.

It was a drizzly Seattle afternoon. Her day off, and she had a half-dozen things to do: homework, reading for Nora's class, martial arts practice, sifting apartment listings. Instead, here she was, dodging puddles. However un-Seat-tleite it was, she'd brought an umbrella.

Two blocks from the house, a silhouette told her she was being followed.

In glances, shielding her gaze with the umbrella, she looked back.

Seeing that muscle daddy look, bulky under a leather jacket, she wanted to kick herself.

She could double back, but these side streets were too empty. The back alleys were worse, tight between fences lined with trash bins.

Picking up her pace, she jog-walked to the main drag. She'd get to the drugstore, get what she needed, get a soda and swallow some ibuprofen, and wait for Cleo to pick her up.

She ran to the end of the street to make the light—flat out the last bit, leaping a puddle.

Only after she'd put a block between them did she look back, a river of traffic separating them, shielding herself from his view with her umbrella.

She was right. It was Max.

She took a fast pace to the drugstore, not quite running.

Within its heavy glass door, she shut her umbrella, shook it, and folded it up.

Her hands kept shaking after closing the umbrella. Finding the restroom, she shut herself into a stall.

She was trembling all over. She was sick to her stomach. Also she was angry.

Couldn't she go anywhere now?

Why was he even like this? Why did he care so much? Mark's death was a horrible accident. Her boyfriend had died too.

She breathed in and out, trying to find calm. She kept shaking.

Chapter 21

*I*n her basement room, a week later, she turned the space heater on, sat a moment before the red bars of warmth. She needed to be warm for this process.

It might not work. The kind of experience she had at Imbolc rarely repeated.

She walked herself down the black marble steps, past the gilt candelabra. Longing came around the corner like a desert wind, the wind of his space.

When she got there, it was empty and dark, an overcast, opaque night.

A wind tossed up a tiny cyclone, then another, leading her forward. In front of a stand of palm trees sat a bench, sand worked deep into the patterns of the wood. She took a seat.

The loneliness of the place crept up on her.

Maybe she should go look for him.

There was enough ambient light—lamps in the low buildings, starlight, perhaps a hidden moon—that going forward she could find a path between the torches, now burnt out. Sand drifted across it, but she pushed tiny dunes aside with her foot.

The pavilion was dark, and she hesitated, but after a moment found the door and pushed through.

Pale light suffused the interior, she couldn't tell from where.

The bed was mussed, coverlet thrown off, tossed on the ground. A heavy smell of blood hung in the air, like meat.

Coming forward, she saw the sheets were dense, wet, pooled with blood. She took a quick breath in. The bed was empty.

A trail of blood led to the corner of the tent. She pushed through a second door, a billow of cloth.

The trail went into trackless desert.

If she followed the trail, even if she got lost in the desert, eventually she'd wake up in her bed.

Step by step, she followed blood droplets, plentiful then thinning out. Once she let her eyes adjust, she found enough light. Now and again, she looked back to make sure the way. Fires glowed on the far side of the pavilion she'd left.

Cresting a rise, she stopped abruptly, scrambling backward. Chunks of dirt fell.

A huge drop-off faced her.

Cliffs of black basalt went down, down, down. No vegetation, it was a rip in the world, lined with stone.

Far away, a cry of pain rang out—human or animal, she couldn't tell.

She was in visionary space. She called for light. The diffuse light intensified.

The chasm went hundreds, thousands of feet down, its black-red rock in shadow, sheer, unclimbable.

Upside down, chained to the basalt with massive, rusted iron bands, hung a body. Its black wings were torn, broken, bloody. Gashes went through the wings, into his back, built on a map of earlier scars.

She felt it as if her own flesh was torn. His face pressed against the rocks.

Whatever was written, this was wrong.

This was a vision. She could fly if she wanted.

Drifting down like a feather, she came to him, her head level with his.

Seeing her, he started.

"Sweetheart," she said, bringing her mouth to his. His lips were cracked and dry. "How can I help you?"

"Water." His voice was a croak.

She materialized a cup of water, fed him small sips, upside down.

"What is this? You were unbound."

"Penance."

He meant for his rebellion, so long ago.

"You never gave in."

"No." He'd never formally repented to the Demiurge—he would not bend the knee. Some of the Watchers perhaps were free, not him.

"What can I do to change this?"

"If I had known you would be here, this is not what you would see. Here."

A wind blew up, full of dust. She coughed, pushed backward. Then his hand cupped her waist, his arm slid around her, and they flew upward.

"But you're still chained."

"Always. But I am also spirit."

When he set her on her feet behind the pavilion, the blood trail was gone.

They entered, the candles on the candelabra lighting themselves. Past the bed was a low couch and grey-black table, she thought ebony, decorated with gilt. He settled on the couch and patted the space next to him. His wings had disappeared. She sat.

Before them, a silver pitcher stood, vines embossed on it, two cups. It amused her a spirit would drink wine. He raised an eyebrow; she nodded; he poured her a cup.

She couldn't get the bound figure with ripped black wings out of her mind.

"You're always there."

"It is my lot."

"You will be freed someday."

He shrugged. "I was saying to your—how do you think of them? Spirit-guide? I seek freedom not especially for myself. I have my path and affordances. I wish to free my people."

The tents and buildings, the lamps and firelight—that was his legions' space.

"How can I help you?"

"There is a way to help, which is why I came to you and Puabi-Ekur. It is given to humans to seek release for their dead, also other spirits, ascension from one plane to the next. However, time and again humans who cared for me or my people went to the Demiurge and were denied that release. I wish now to take another path."

"How does that work?"

"So far it does not. Before we go much further, I should

tell you a story."

Refilling her cup, he told the tale of Saadiya and her cousin Zivah.

"This is what I remember you from, the first time, from my dream."

"Yes. It is some of my earliest history, just after I chose to be embodied."

"You've told this story to Puabi-Ekur?"

"Yes. I believe they also remember it."

Joanie grinned. "So, you and Puabi-Ekur...?" She gestured.

He shook his head.

"Some incubus-succubus! You got me to put out, at least." Her own first encounter with Puabi-Ekur had been sex, the spirit then in Clayton's body.

"I need you both for this practice. As I say, we've tried the trodden path. We appealed to the Demiurge and were rejected. My hope is to go to the earlier deities. Puabi-Ekur has long history with Inanna and Ereshkigal."

"And I'm human."

"Just so."

The walls of the black pavilion shifted with the wind. Candlelight fell on the planes of his face, the edge of his lip cut like stone. She sipped her wine, keeping her face down to hide her expression.

It hadn't been about her at all.

"So none of this is just for old times' sake."

"I would not say that."

She slipped forward on the couch and brushed back from his face his long, curling black hair. He took her face in his hands and kissed her.

The longing entwined them both.

"But you're this angel, this Witch-father. You must have relationships with so many people."

A corner of his lip quirked up.

"Remember only heathens and apostates come to me. And yet they must believe. The subset of those to whom I used to be married is small." He kissed her again. "Very small."

She climbed across his lap, smiling to feel him hard beneath her.

It didn't matter who paid back whom.

She rocked back and forth. Molten fire welled upward through her. He took her hands and leaned forward, kissing her, nipping her.

"I'm in. I guess we'll have to talk Puabi-Ekur into it."

"I do not think they trust me."

She looked back along the long years, the string of beads.

Images of a medieval life fell before her eyes, like a sheaf of dropped photographs: a blue linen dress, a wooden floor, a half-tester bed. Even in that life, he'd appeared as a vignette. Perhaps then she'd called him to her. To do what? Some infernal errand? The images flew away.

She got no sense Azazel had broken agreements.

"Maybe that's mostly about them."

"Perhaps."

He pulled her closer and bit her neck. Tonguing down the tendon, he licked her collarbone, took her nipple in his teeth through her loose gown.

"Perhaps I should have come back more often. But I am here now."

Chapter 22

$\mathcal{P}$uabi-Ekur lay a long time flung in front of Hekate's empty throne.

The stars cycled. The braziers smoked; the torches burned.

It was clear what the goddess had to say by not speaking. It was not Puabi-Ekur's time to go on.

They had been free a long time, but they were committed now. Azazel would let them slip the chain, but their agreement was to Hekate.

To let go now—they could fall infinitely, but each step down made it harder to rise, or to change. For love's sake, they'd decided to change.

They hovered in the aether, among the stars, out of time and space, sitting with this.

Something kept tugging them back to the oasis.

After a while, they figured it out.

Angry and disgruntled, feeling dragged, though dragged by themself, they winged to the black-red chasm where

Azazel hung, bloody, chained to the basalt with rusted iron bands.

They appeared beside him with cup and pitcher.

They did not put on the body of Puabi, or any body at all, but rather appeared as wind.

"Greetings, most fair."

"Drink the fucking water."

Azazel laughed.

Chapter 23

*N*ora's third class had been pushed out by an unseasonable snow. Now folks gathered, on pillows on the wood-laminate floor of the yurt. Joanie and Cleo eyed the group. Of the seven who'd started the class, the three from Nora's coven were missing.

Entering, Nora threw a pillow down at the height of the group's arc.

"Olivia and your other coven members—they're not coming anymore?" Cleo asked.

Nora's lips pressed together, keeping in Joanie wasn't sure what; annoyance, perhaps. "Olivia was just auditing. Jackie and Shaun were overbooked. Let's get started."

They described their datura visions from the previous class. Some had seen datura as a plant spirit, one as moonbeams. Some, like Joanie, had seen a beautiful woman.

Alyssa told her story last. Sunrays fell across the floor of the yurt, floating in her white-blonde hair.

"I've been working with Moonshadow as a guide for, I

don't know, maybe six months? They're nonbinary, and they're an angel. They come to me in meditations and give me advice." She looked across at Joanie. "After the Watchers ritual we did, I wondered if there was a connection there. Moonshadow was shy but eventually admitted it."

This was news, but everyone in the coven had a personal practice, and they didn't always discuss details.

"When we called in datura, Moonshadow came in, presenting as femme. Big yellow-white dress, moon energy, as if they were dressed in datura. And they told me to keep them close, that they would watch and protect me. It's the first time I've seen them so clearly!"

She looked across at Joanie.

"They expressed curiosity about you and your spiritual connections." Of course Alyssa had talked to Gus, who knew about Fallen Angel Boyfriend.

"We can talk."

"Sounds as if there's a resonance with your practice," Nora said. "Just as a reminder—if you do work along the poison path, take care. Datura, for example, contains dangerous alkaloids, in particular atropine."

Alyssa raised her hand.

"What does that mean, in practice?"

"Let me read you some details." Nora called up a reference on her phone. "All parts of datura contain dangerous levels of atropine, hyoscyamine, and scopolamine, which are classified as deliriants, or anticholinergics."

She looked up from her phone. "A deliriant makes you delirious—hallucinations and so on. An anticholinergic blocks the action of one of the neurotransmitters that affect how your body functions. For example, you might retain urine if you take too much datura."

She continued reading: "The risk of fatal overdose is high among uninformed users. Negative affects of datura intoxication include hyperthermia, faster than normal heartbeat, bizarre behavior, urinary retention as I said, and severe dilation of the pupils with painful light sensitivity that can last several days."

Alyssa's eyes had gone round.

"Datura is no joke." Nora stood. "With that introduction, let's return to the greenhouse."

Nora led the class out, into an overcast day, warm. Slowly greater Seattle nudged into spring. Against the grey, the grass flared green as emerald.

At the greenhouse's back stood the dark-green shrubs covered with cream-colored flowers, most now shut.

"Collect a double handful of the blooms. Be sure to wear your gloves. Even a small exposure can cause a psychoactive change, and you might be more susceptible than you think. Once you have enough, return to the yurt and grab a mortar and pestle to start macerating them. It helps to tear them up beforehand."

Cleo and Joanie got their datura before the others. On the table lay staged mortars of white marble, paired with pestles. They settled on the floor. Such old work this was, done since before writing—women's work.

Leaning into her girlfriend, Joanie said, "You asked about Nora's coven folks quitting. Hannah said Nora's coven has been dwindling for a while. Jackie's more interested in chaos magic now, and Shaun follows Jackie. Olivia's about ready to hive off. That leaves Nora with, I think, two people besides herself."

Something nudged at Joanie, a gap she could fill. She had always loved Nora's farm, a witch farm, where earth spirits and witches met in harmony. She had dreamed of a witch farm.

The other class members came in, trailed by Nora.

"The flowers aren't going to take much maceration. Once they're in shreds, you can add them to the alcohol."

Chapter 24

A slow night passed at the coffee shop. Steady rain fell against the windows, stitches of light traced against black. Joanie finished all her work in back, then mopped.

Gus was the only one there, nursing his coffee and doing homework on his laptop. Having finished the scutwork, Joanie came to sit with him.

"Thanks again for watching out for me."

"I'm just surprised Max isn't trying to attack me. I'm the betrayer ex."

Joanie cocked her head. "You still wish he cared."

"That would be a poor way of showing it, granted."

"You said he used to be something of an intellectual. Now he's acting like a hired killer. Though maybe it's vengeance."

"One of the last things he said to me was that he wanted to be just. Either way, this doesn't seem just."

"I'm sure he's been on a journey. I don't know much

about the European far right, but I imagine it's as much of an echo chamber as it is here."

"I still thought he was better than this."

At closing time, she locked the door, counted the money, and prepped the drop bag for the bank.

"Let's take the long way home tonight, despite the rain. Every time we take it easy, I feel nervous."

The bank drop-off slot was only a few blocks down. Having visited it, they headed north, scoping left and right for threats.

Black night, shining streets—at a corner, puddles reflected the red of the stoplight. The rain had let up. Water still hung heavy in the air, but only a few drops condensed from mist.

"Let's cross over here, then go up Brooklyn for a while."

Brooklyn was a central, high-traffic, brightly lit street, a nod to safety.

Not too far along, footsteps sounded behind them.

Joanie and Gus glanced at each other, then back.

Two men, both bulky, were silhouetted against white street light. Their heavy, stalking footsteps said predators.

"Let's run the rest of it," Joanie said.

They took off, barreling down the narrow sidewalk, dodging passers-by and jutting bushes, leaping uneven pavement.

From a side street, two men jumped out, running full-tilt, cutting off their way forward. The two men turned to face them.

The men behind closed in.

Gus nodded ahead, to their next move: "Both of us on puffy coat guy."

Running up, Gus socked him. A lucky hit knocked the man sideways at Joanie. Two-handed, she punched down on the side of his head, sending him to the ground.

He grabbed her ankle, and she was down. Hot pain flared in her arm. Wriggling wildly, she kicked him in the balls. He let go, clutching his crotch.

Gus chopped the other guy in the throat. He dropped back, choking.

Scrambling up, Joanie ran. Gus followed close.

The men from behind didn't stop for the fallen but ran, chasing Gus and Joanie. They had a good lead. Again the gods of traffic smiled on Joanie. The men kept a steady pace behind.

Six blocks to go.

Five blocks to go. "Let's go over to Twelfth Street."

Crossing the dark side street, they sprinted down the middle, splashing.

Four blocks. A car pulled out of a parking space. They veered into the street to avoid it. The men trailing them had to stop.

Three blocks. Maybe they'd make it.

Two, one.

Half a block from Firebird House, the street narrow and quiet, a couple of men stepped out from a bank of laurel bushes.

One was Max.

Fuck.

But only half a block was left.

Gus glanced at Joanie. They should swarm not Max but the other, smaller dude, in a lumberjack-check flannel shirt.

Running in, Gus shoulder-blocked him.

The guy didn't go down, but Joanie got past.

She couldn't leave Gus.

The two men punched each other, Max circling.

Max, all muscle, punched in, hard. Gus grunted as he took the hit. It had to hurt.

Grabbing the closest trash bin, she rolled it into them.

All three men went down, the smaller guy rolling and moaning. Gus popped up. He ran past, splashing in a big puddle.

With a scramble and reach, Max grabbed Joanie. Pulling a knife, he put the blade to her throat.

Cold steel seared her flesh. Her body froze against her will.

She was going to die.

"Help! Fire! Fire!" Gus yelled.

Puabi-Ekur! Azazel!

Running, from up the street, the two closest guys grabbed Gus.

A light turned on in one of the houses, nothing more.

Joanie twisted in Max's grip, but he held her fast.

He stared at Gus.

"I could just kill her now. But I won't." To the man in the lumberjack shirt, now climbing to his feet, he said, "Go get the truck."

Something inside her was shrieking.

He wasn't going to kill her fast now. He was going to kill her slowly later.

A wind twisted among the trees, shaking black branches.

"I should have figured I'd see you here," Max said to Gus.

Gus writhed in his captors' grasp. "Why are you doing this?"

"You wouldn't understand, oath-breaker."

Gus growled. "Try me."

"Mark Walker supported us—he helped build our hof. He was a great and good man, like a father to me. I looked up to him."

Joanie snorted.

Max clapped his hand over her mouth. She couldn't get purchase to bite.

"It hurt everyone when you had him killed, you witch. I prayed to Odin to grant vengeance, and he did. When I give you to the god, Mark will smile in Valhalla."

Then, from behind, down the street toward the house, came the pump and click of a pump-action shotgun.

A shot, then another rang out. The bullets went into the bushes.

Cleo advanced down the middle of the street, a couple Firebird House folks beside her.

She pumped the shotgun again, filling the chamber.

"What the *fuck* did you say about killing my girlfriend?"

Gus dropped out of his captors' slackened grip, hitting the street hard. He leaped up and ran to the Firebird House group. Joanie tried the same maneuver, but Max held tight.

Cleo shot the street, still advancing.

"Let go of her. Now."

"Or you're going to kill me?"

"Or you're going to jail," said Joe, coming up beside her. He held his cellphone high, recording. "We have all of this on camera."

Max and his henchman traded a look.

Several more Firebird House people stepped forward.

Across the street, a door opened. "What's going on?"

Joanie felt Max sigh.

He released her. She almost fell.

Stumbling forward, she ran to the Firebird House group.

A white truck rolled up, and the driver threw open the passenger-side door. Max jumped in; the others followed. With a splash of gutter water, the truck drove off.

Joanie made her way to the sidewalk, breathing hard.

"Fuck! Thanks, everyone."

"We have plenty of footage of his assholery," said Joe. "And his license plate number."

"We can get a no-contact order," Gus said. "Maybe assault."

Joanie leaned over, hands propped on knees, staring at the concrete of the sidewalk.

Blood trickled down her neck from the nick where the knife had been. She put her hand to it. It stung. Her arm hurt. The adrenaline wearing off, she felt the pain.

A wisp of wind circled her, caressed her cheek, then whirled away.

"Joanie." Cleo came up, stroking her back and hair. "Joanie. It's over. He's gone."

Chapter 25

Puabi-Ekur! Azazel!

"I will kill him," Azazel said.

He propelled himself off the wall of basalt—or part of him did.

Manifesting larger than Puabi-Ekur had ever seen him, he flung out his wings, full-feathered, black as midnight. His chest shone in his bronze breastplate, his war-kilt studded leather. Slung from its shoulder harness hung his sheathed sword.

"Let's," said Puabi-Ekur, still formless, a fragment, a thought.

They cut into Joanie's reality. A wind shuffled tree branches.

Shoulders squared, Cleo walked forward. She raised her gun.

"Hold," Azazel said.

They watched the scene unfold.

As a wisp of wind, Puabi-Ekur circled Joanie, caressed her cheek, then whirled away.

Azazel sliced out of Joanie's world, back to the pocket hell of the oasis. Wings hidden, wearing his loose dark-red robe, he seated himself on the bench by the palm trees. Puabi-Ekur followed, shifting to Puabi, in a similar black robe.

The grey-blue eyes, lined in black, studied her.

"It is good that Saadiya has strong allies to protect her."

"Cleo has always been that."

"On this, we are aligned, then—on protecting Saadiya."

Puabi sighed.

"We are aligned in general. I accepted your contract. But I am unused to princes among spirit-folk. Hekate is one thing. She is the World Soul; all of us bow to her. But you're different. I gave up being pushed around by men millennia ago."

"Have I, as you put it, pushed you around?"

"No. This is my problem, not yours."

His gaze lay on her face, gentle, stroking the line of her forehead and her cheek, brushing her long crimped hair, as palpable as a touch.

"My flower, I can wait. I have the patience of the damned."

Puabi-Ekur backed out of that reality, into whirling, empty space.

Why were they being such an asshole to Azazel?

They didn't have to be.

He wasn't demanding sex. No one was getting forced.

It wasn't like sex would be a hardship. It was Puabi-Ekur's work, and furthermore Azazel was the most beautiful male they'd ever seen.

The longing from the past remained also, held back like a flood by a dam.

Besides all that, she'd agreed to a contract—as sacred a thing as there was, among spirits. Though it complicated things.

All this together, somehow it was easiest to appear beside Azazel as a disembodied spirit with a cup and pitcher.

The unending red-black basalt wall reached down and down, to the center of the earth.

Azazel turned toward them, eyes unreadable, and drank, small sips, one by one.

Chapter 26

*A*fter the truck pulled away, the residents of Firebird House filed inside to have their last group argument under the sunflower paintings.

"In principle, at least, we started as a house of anarchists," Casey said. "We consciously separate ourselves from the police state. We can't turn around and use the police."

"We, as a group, are breaking up," said Joe. "Joanie, as a human, has a right to protect herself from assault. I for one am happy to use the footage I took to help her do that."

In the end, Joe's stance won—no one denied him the right to share the footage he'd taken.

"I think we'll have to report to the police, but I'm more than willing to do that," he said. "We should do that right away."

"Sure, let's," Joanie said. She dialed 9-1-1.

It took the police several hours to get there. There was a snag about Cleo's using the shotgun, but with her being registered to use the weapon, given all the witnesses, and the fact the only shooting victims were the grass and the street, the police let it go.

"Even a Black woman gets to stand her ground," Joe said.

With Max, the video footage of him holding a knife against Joanie's throat was plenty to prove their point. They would file charges for assault and at the same time start a no-contact order in motion. For that, after the police report, Joanie's next step was to fill out the forms required, then go before a judge. She'd do the first of these in the morning.

Cleo insisted Joanie sleep in her bed, wrapping her in her arms. Exhausted, Joanie went to sleep quickly, only to be tangled in dream.

Trapped in black night, she froze, knife-blade to her throat.

She woke with a start.

Her hand went to the cut on her neck, cleaned and bandaged, still stinging.

Tears prickled her lids, from old, old fear.

Her movement woke Cleo.

"Oh, baby." She petted Joanie's hair and skin. "Ssh. It's okay now."

The apartment they found was a compromise. Centrally located, it was in range of Nora's and the U District, a short jaunt north of the covenstead, and on a bus route. If you squinted, you could call the tiny second room a bedroom.

"It can be an office, and we can keep the futon folded up most of the time," Joanie said.

Joanie had considered asking Nora if she had places at the farm, which she ran with live-in help. But she didn't feel ready. She barely knew Nora, and Nora and Hannah had dicey history—she didn't want to rile her high priestess. The farm was also far away from the city and would be a lot of work.

The larger room they made Cleo's; Cleo would squeeze her desk into it, and they'd share the bed. Joanie took the smaller bedroom as office and ritual room. They could pull out the futon for guests.

It was in a townhouse in a group built in the nineties, its walls and fixtures all white. Outside, the buildings showed a range of tans from the era of mushroom colors. Most of the residents were young couples and small families.

"If we don't like it, we can look again in a year," Cleo said.

"Maybe space will come open in Hannah's house."

For Firebird House, time was up. By the time Cleo and Joanie started packing, many of the residents had already gone, though the couches still sat in the living room.

Boxes, files, books, dishes, furniture—luckily, thanks to living small, they didn't have that much. They rented a truck and barely filled half of it. Only the long furniture made it a requirement.

Returning, they cleaned Joanie's basement niche and Cleo's upstairs nook.

Then, sitting on one of the couches, Cleo slid their keys into an envelope, closed it, and tossed it onto the living room coffee table.

"I remember when I first moved in," Cleo said. She'd

been there six years, a true believer. "They threw me a party. With this tiny cake. Cosima baked it. She's long gone now—she moved to Massachusetts to work for a union. So many people have come and gone, but I thought the core would live. I thought the house would live."

She covered her face with her hands, tears trickling down.

"Oh, Cleo." Joanie kissed her wet cheek. "Nothing lives forever."

"Community doesn't go away. If not Firebird House, Firebird Community. If not Firebird Community, something else."

Joanie wouldn't miss the arguments of the past year, but things had once been better. Forum had once worked to allay group tensions.

A few stalwarts planned a weekly dinner at Joe's place—he was moving to a different U District community house. Joanie had agreed vaguely, not sure if she wanted to join.

Cleo sniffled. Joanie retrieved some toilet paper, and she blew her nose.

They pulled the door shut behind them, letting it lock. The spring day overcast had breaks of blue. Across the street, the first daffodils bloomed.

They climbed into the cab of the rented truck, cold vinyl seat under blue-jeaned legs, going forward. Joanie felt better going forward.

Besides everything else, it was safer, at least for her.

Chapter 27

The datura tincture sat lined up in bottles in a shadowy metal cabinet. Nora let each student take theirs out, to check and gloat. In a clear glass bottle, Joanie's was pale green.

"We could technically use it now, since it's been a couple of weeks, but I generally let mine sit at least a month. Again, be very careful in its use. Never, ever, for example, just drink the tincture. I never use it except as an ingredient in my flying ointment, which is applied topically—you'd have to do a lot of work to poison yourself with it. And with the ointment, always pretest before sharing it."

When Joanie opened hers, what she smelled was alcohol.

"Before we move on to something we're going to work with, let's talk about mandrake, perhaps the most famous of witch herbs. Mandrake roots look like miniature human beings, so they were used for love potions and poppet work. Mandrake also has hallucinogenic and anesthetic properties, so it was used in ancient times to knock people out for surgery. But mandrake is notoriously hard to grow. I've had some limited success. I add mine to my flying ointment."

Nora walked them over to the greenhouse to meet the mandrake plants, with fluted dark-green leaves, a few showing purple flowers.

"In legend, mandrake would scream when pulled from the ground, and the scream was fatal. Mandrake definitely has a strong spirit, and I know a number of witches who work with it. Even though we're not going to try to grow it for class, I want to give you the opportunity to meet it in visionary space."

She collected a potted mandrake. Back in the yurt, she had the students lie down, lowering the shades to shut out spring sunshine. Joanie grabbed a pillow. The floor lay cool beneath.

"You're becoming more and more relaxed…"

Nora talked them into trance. A being showed up for Joanie—not like her image of mandrake, rather a white-clad spirit, in filmy material, perhaps with wings, but those weren't clear. The spirit reminded her of Alyssa's Moonshadow. Joanie hadn't had a chance to talk to Alyssa about Moonshadow—they'd both been busy.

Filmy gossamer clothing draped a slender, tall, androgynous body. Long hair fell pale as moonbeams across silvergrey eyes. The mandrake spirit, a dark, shrubby homunculus, hunkered in the background.

"Are you the one Alyssa calls Moonshadow?"

"Yes, your friend calls me Moonshadow. I have many names."

Many angels had multiple names—perhaps like the fey they were loath to give their true names.

"She said you had connections to the Watcher angels."

"I was with them on Mount Hebron, when they first came down to Earth. Our paths have separated since. Are you one that is allied with Azazel?"

A hint of doubt whispered to be cautious here. But she saw no reason not to speak.

"I am."

"I have not seen Azazel for millennia. I was one like Samyaza."

"Samyaza repented." Formally, to the Demiurge, she presumed.

"Yes."

Yet Azazel and Samyaza were still close, or so she'd taken from the stories.

In a vague, half-lit aetheric space, the angel drifted closer. There was something narcotic about their presence, like a dream. Though Joanie had read Moonshadow as femme, their wiry shoulders and arms were masculine, or at least strong-muscled.

The angel closed on her, staring.

"You are lovers, with Azazel."

"We hooked up."

The angel floated out a hand, then retracted it.

"I was Azazel's lover, long ago. Much I regret in my past, but not that."

"You miss him."

"Yes. I regret how we separated."

They emanated a glowing fog, like moonlight. Luminous silver-grey eyes shone in their long, high-cheekboned face. The pale hair swirled as if underwater.

"I'm sorry. Shall I pass on a message?"

"Do not tell him of me, please. It was long ago. We parted badly."

A flash of sorrow crossed the long face.

"Tell me of him. What are his actions, his loves now?"

Joanie never trusted anyone quickly, particularly spirits, who chose how they appeared. But she didn't want to deny Moonshadow information—she wanted to be kind.

"He is trapped in his pocket hell, Dudael. He does magic. He reached out to me and my spirit-guide—"

"The little succubus?"

A tentative wisp entered her mind and was sorting through her memories.

"Excuse me, don't do that."

A mist came down between them, a fog of moonlight. It softened edges. The wisp didn't leave.

She shoved her energetic self backward, hard.

"Stop it, please."

The angel widened their silver eyes.

"I'm going to end this conversation."

She sent a wave of cobalt-blue flame, pushing out everything that wasn't her. A few blasts shoved Moonshadow away.

She called Hekate for good measure: *Hekate, Queen of Angels, help me.*

A scent of garlic filled her nose, and her space was clear. She put a wall of blue flame around her.

She sat up, shaking her head. Everyone else still lay in trance, strewn across the laminate floor on pillows.

Nora came over. "Are you okay?"

"Now I am."

"Let me run some energy for you. Mandrake can be intense."

It hadn't been mandrake, but she wanted to sort things out before she talked about her experience. The backstory was too complex to tell Nora in a hurry. Closing her eyes, she let Nora run a short guided meditation in whispers, filling her with golden light. It couldn't hurt.

She didn't talk to Alyssa about Moonshadow on the way home, afraid Cleo would blame Alyssa for the spirit's encroachment. She stayed after work at the coffee shop the next afternoon to catch Alyssa at her break—Alyssa worked there too.

In the spring day, clouds like white cotton candy glided across the blue sky. Between them, rays cascaded down to splash across the room. She got her usual cappuccino and pulled out her accounting homework.

Not touching it, she stared into the blue.

She'd known Alyssa three years. She'd helped the girl escape her pimp; she'd helped her find a home. Alyssa had joined the coven and proved to be a natural medium and witch. She was like a younger sister.

With a thump, Alyssa threw herself down into the booth across from her. She'd brought a macchiato.

"What's up? You wanted to talk."

"You told me about your spirit Moonshadow. When we meditated with mandrake, I got a little bit of mandrake but a lot of Moonshadow. They were really in my space, kind of pushy."

Alyssa took a sip of her coffee.

"They were a bit like that with me to start, but they stopped when I set boundaries."

Would Alyssa have noticed if Moonshadow continued tagging along places or riffling through her memories?

"They seem like someone to be careful with—like if you set boundaries they might try to circumvent them secretly. I had to do extra work to get rid of them. I called in Hekate."

"I'm sorry. Maybe I should do more."

Likely, but Joanie didn't want to push the point too hard.

"I can tell they offended you. I can ask them to apologize."

"It wouldn't hurt, but also, they seemed really interested in Azazel—my angel friend. Too interested. I ended up feeling suspicious, like they were stalking him."

Alyssa rubbed her hands over her face.

"I'm sorry. They didn't say a word of that to me. You think I should stop working with them?" She looked as if about to burst into tears. "Maybe I'm just being dumb. Maybe I shouldn't be doing any of this."

"I didn't say that. But there's stuff to learn at all points of this path."

"I've been talking to Hannah."

"Let's ask Hannah what she thinks." Hannah could help navigate this. Possibly, with a primer, Moonshadow could get better about consent, although they'd been told by Alyssa and still didn't pay attention to Joanie. Also Alyssa would take instruction better from Hannah.

Part of her wanted to tell Azazel immediately. But Azazel had powerful protection—he was in no danger.

Chapter 28

Cleo had gone to sleep. In her ritual room, Joanie sat down to meditate.

So far, the decor was boxes and her makeshift table. The futon sat folded against the wall, under a black throw. She'd set out the coral-pink candle on its small plate as her focus point.

Deeper and deeper she went, drifting and focusing.

After a time, she settled on the sand-embedded bench at the oasis, watched by a sardonic angel. Stars pinpricked blue-black night, dimmed by lamplight from nearby buildings.

In his long red kilt, he draped himself gracefully as a big cat. Half-hidden wings fell as shadows behind him. Those muscled shoulders—she wanted to bite them. His dark frankincense scent drew her in.

She rocked on her haunches, feeling like a cat in heat. He could just prop her against one of the trees. That'd be fine.

A corner of his lip quirked. He could tell what she

wanted. To start, he offered wine. The glint from a far lantern licked the pitcher's silver skin.

"My lily, my flowering branch, tell me about this evil man who pursues you, this Max."

She told the story, and he sipped and watched her.

When she finished, he reached out and cupped her cheek. She closed her eyes, and he bent forward, kissed her, then sat back. The kiss brought tears to her eyes.

"You will not be able to concentrate on much more than self-protection until he is gone."

"I suppose that's true."

"I shall kill him."

"Wait a moment. I don't—"

"Persuade me he is not an entirely worthless human."

His eyes were the color of the sky just before sunrise, limpid and merciless.

"Has he not caused the death of others, and for no reason other than his whim? Now he intends to kill you."

She released a breath.

Max meant to murder her. The legal system was set to fail her.

If she had to choose, she chose herself.

He picked up her hand and kissed her palm.

"He will have his chance to defeat me. He can call in patrons. You say he is a pious man, of a sort."

She climbed into his lap, stroked his shoulder, kissed it, laid her cheek on it. His scent enveloped her. She sniffled a little and rubbed her wet cheek on him.

He wrapped her tight in his arms, kissing her hair.

"He is not worth a single one of your tears."

At Hannah's small dining table, at the end of her narrow railroad kitchen, she sat with Joanie and Alyssa over tea.

"I'd like some background on how this Moonshadow spirit showed up."

Alyssa shifted in her chair.

"I've been working with them for maybe six months. They weren't always good about boundaries, but after a couple of discussions they backed off on that, for me. Like they were in my head a lot, and I had to push them out. I threatened to cut ties with them, and they chilled out."

She looked at Joanie helplessly.

"They bring me good luck. They're good at finding things, putting them in my path, especially moon stuff." She pulled forward the lapel of her black denim jacket. "See this little moon pin? I found it just after talking to them. They said they were an angel, and nonbinary. But they kind of felt fey to me."

"So you had no reason to doubt their good intentions."

"No. Like I say, they were pretty pushy up front, but that stopped."

Hannah inclined her head a moment, considering, before turning to Joanie.

"But your experience was different."

She'd filled Hannah in. "Yeah. We talked before about Fallen Angel Boyfriend. Moonshadow said they had an old connection with him, which ended badly. They were hung up on that."

Hannah tilted her head, gazing at Joanie.

"Something can be good for one person and bad for

another. Joanie, I think you were right to shield. Alyssa, if I were in your shoes I'd do some divination, maybe talk to Hekate."

"Sure, I can." Alyssa frowned. "How can you tell if a spirit is not what they seem?"

"What I'm suggesting generally works for me. If you have long-term spirit guides or another deity you trust, ask them what they think."

"But we talked, and I did that, and they backed off!" She flopped down over the table.

Hannah stroked her pale blonde hair. "Spirits can be sneaky and bide their time. No harm in checking again."

"Okay, okay. I will." To Joanie, she said, "You know I didn't mean any harm."

"Of course not. But it's like Hannah said. Spirits can be sneaky."

Maybe Moonshadow had somehow seen all this coming, had been waiting for an opportunity to get at Azazel. She should tell him.

Chapter 29

Gus hunkered in the coffee shop corner, doing his homework. A heavy rain fell, sluicing through the streets. In the windy night, gusts hit the windows in thumps.

Since he was the only customer, Joanie sat with him after her tasks were done.

"I thought you were moving to daytime shifts?"

"I can't yet. They conflict with my classes."

"He's going to find out where you live."

"We put up the cameras at the new place today."

"It's still not as much protection as at Firebird House. Or my house."

"Maybe I can crash downstairs at your place sometimes."

Gus grimaced. "I'm afraid he'll target Cleo. I think you both should stay over."

Gus was right, but tonight she'd made plans to drive home—to her new home, which she wasn't interested in abandoning for Max Dwyer.

"I told Cleo I'd be home tonight. It's a bit late to change my mind."

"Okay, but pass on my suggestion, okay?"

"I will."

At the end of her shift, he walked her to her car, going the long way and checking to make sure they weren't followed. Streetlight showed white tracings of rain against the night.

"I'll drop you home." It was a little out of her way, but she wanted to make sure he didn't get attacked by Max for helping her.

At the covenstead, daffodils stood in ranks, golden trumpets shut for night.

Before he got out, Gus said, "Be careful till you're in company. Call in our mutual friend." He meant Puabi-Ekur.

"Good idea."

Puabi-Ekur! Azazel! Be with me tonight.

After dropping Gus off, she got on the highway going north. Bright winking white headlights and a red glitter of taillights slipped by, washed and broken up by rain. Water on the road hissed and splashed, the beat of her windshield wipers steady. Occasionally, big gusts pushed hard enough to nudge the car sideways.

She turned off again. The townhouse development sat along a main road, but threading the parking lot to her building she still sometimes got lost. Perhaps it was silly, but as she pulled in she called Cleo.

"I'm driving into the parking lot. If I don't show up shortly, you might need to come find me."

As it turned out, she found parking under a carport fifty yards from her place. She got out, locked the car. For now, the rain had stopped. Beside the white-painted trellis, a box held a few daffodils, bright yellow. A gust of wind tossed them; the scent of wet bark hung in the air.

A few dozen feet of sidewalk and a half-flight of stairs lay between her and the apartment.

Just before her building, Max lurched out from behind a maple tree.

He must have followed her from the coffee shop.

After a moment of pure, shocked stillness, she spun on her heel and ran.

She ran along a parking lot puddled with rain. She turned a corner, then turned again, trying to lose him. Her heart beat staccato.

She fled flat-out across a sea of wet asphalt and dove through a narrow space between buildings, black, smelling of garbage.

She popped out onto the sidewalk, footsteps not far behind.

There was her sidewalk, her flight of steps.

Her door opened to a halo of light.

With her shotgun, Cleo stepped down the half-flight. She pumped the gun, chambering a round. Joanie scrambled up beside her.

Seeing Cleo, Max stopped.

"Did you not get the point last time?" Cleo asked. "Get out of here."

He advanced a step, two.

The glare of a streetlight showed his black hoodie and jeans, white t-shirt, big frame, broad rounded shoulders—solid, muscular, frightening.

He could kill Joanie, and he wanted to.

"You wouldn't really shoot me."

"Don't fucking tell me what I'd do."

Cleo's shot rang, ricocheting on asphalt, past his feet.

"Get out of here. Next time I shoot to kill."

He stood in place.

Cleo chambered a bullet. She raised her gun.

She took a step backward, up one stair, gun trained on Max.

She took another step up, Joanie behind her.

Another. The point of the gun moved, and Max leaned forward.

"Stop!"

He froze.

Two more steps, and they were up the stairs. Joanie scrabbled at their door, opened it.

They were through.

They stood a minute or so in the kitchen, arms around each other.

With a squeal of brakes, the white truck flashed past the window and disappeared.

Joanie called the maintenance guy to explain the shots, then Gus, who reassured her he was safe. As she hung up, a wave of exhaustion crashed over her.

"Just one more call, sweetheart. To the police. You have the no-contact order."

That night, in her dream, the oasis stand of palms appeared, the sand-ingrained bench, the darkness painted with yellow light.

Sitting beside her, Azazel put his arm around her, with soft dry lips kissed her cheek. Feathers tickled her skin.

His lips moved from her cheek to her mouth. His fingertips stroked the side of her breast. Then he drew away.

"I have something to show you."

He reached into the air, and with his index finger opened a window.

"Watch."

A white truck went down a Seattle highway, in night and rain. Seen through the driver's window, Max sat in the cab, wearing his black hoodie with a vee of white t-shirt.

He drove fast, passing car after car, cutting too close. Rain lashed down, glittering in street light.

The truck went onto a high bridge, silhouetted against a sweep of grey water and the silver lights of the city, the view filtered by a fence. Wind rattled the fence, shaking the rain like a curtain.

A gust punched the truck, hard enough to push it across a lane, then two. It ricocheted off the concrete barrier, spun and stopped, horizontal across two lanes.

Cars screeched to a halt.

Another gust tipped the truck onto the driver's side.

Another picked the truck up a foot, then slammed it down, crushing it.

The driver's side window shattered, safety glass splattering outward. The metal frame flattened, dark inside.

Across the bent metal of the window frame flowed black blood. A hand fell out through the broken glass.

$\mathcal{M}$ax was dead.

Next to her on the bench, Azazel stroked her hair.

"This disturbs you, flower of my heart."

"I just wanted him to stop harassing me."

"That was not going to happen while he lived. Now he is facing himself, as it is right for him to do."

On the bridge, people crowded around the truck. A siren blared in the distance, emergency vehicles on their way.

"It's so final. Maybe he could have changed his path."

"He tried to kidnap and kill you several times. I told you I would kill him."

"People say that kind of thing all the time."

"With angels, word and deed are very close." He frowned, looking at her under his eyebrows. "Did you not want him dead?"

"I don't go around wanting people dead." She took a

deep breath, let it out. "But I did choose. I chose me, not him. What happens now?"

"He cleans up any unfinished business, as he can. Then it depends on what he believes." He kissed her cheek. "Death is certainly not the end."

Standing, he reached down and took her hand.

"Come, let me change your mood."

The torches that led to the pavilion were lit, flames swaying.

She woke to her white bedroom, white curtains drifting, full of light. They hadn't decorated yet.

Her phone beeped, a text from Gus.

<Did you see what happened?>

He linked to a newscast. Someone had gotten video that showed the truck crash.

Joanie texted: <Do you have a little time to talk?>

<Just leaving class. I'll call in 5>

Cleo was off at work. Joanie sat up, stretched, sipped water from the glass on the bedside table, propped herself against the headboard.

The phone rang.

"Was that not fucking intense? It looks as if that truck—"

"Yeah, I know. You know that ritual we did, a while back, to the Watcher angels?"

"Yeah?"

"I got a special friend out of it."

"We talked about this. Fallen Angel Boyfriend. It sounded sexy."

"He asked me what the point of Max was. I honestly couldn't tell him. I thought about it. If it was him or me, I picked me. Next thing I knew, this happened."

"Whoa."

"I know. But, in the end… it kind of was him or me. It means I owe the angel a favor, but I was going to do what he wanted anyway."

"I will say, no one in mundane life is going to pin this on an angel. They'll just call it a freak wind or some kind of accident."

"Odin's Hunt might know what's up—that we're witches, and fighting them."

"Those were Hunt guys supporting Max, when he jumped us by Firebird House. But if they think it's witchcraft, they're just going to be—well, freaked out and impressed. I'm freaked out and impressed."

"How do you feel, though? Now Max is dead."

"Alyssa asked me that. I don't feel much. I lost Max a long time ago."

They traded good-byes. She stared at her phone, set it aside when it went dark.

She hadn't crashed the truck herself, but someone was dead because of her. However often he'd tried to kill her, that was still true.

Getting up, she went into her office and lit a tealight, putting it on her altar.

"May his way be clear. May he get what needs in the next life."

Azazel had reassured her death was not the end.

She wanted it to be the end with her and Max. He'd make a nasty ghost.

Chapter 31

*P*alm leaves shifted in the evening breeze, against a sky shades of dark blue but for a line of raw sienna at the horizon.

Puabi-Ekur sat, in Puabi form, in black, all shadow, back against the rough palm bark, elbows on knees and hands hanging forward. A pool of lamplight from the nearest building reached out but didn't touch her.

Azazel approached from the tents, breeze ruffling his long hair, again in his loose red robe.

"You killed him."

"You at least cannot regret that. You gave permission for my hunt—you said, let us do this."

"Will there be no consequences for his death?"

"Look for changes in his Odin's Hunt group."

"But I mean, for you? You're not working for the Demiurge. Surely killing someone affects your fate?"

He threw himself down beside her. A curl of dark hair rested on her shoulder a moment, then fell away.

"You are concerned about my redemption? How sweet."

"I'm not not."

"A most definitive statement."

"Are you teasing me, angel?"

Pushing back a little on the bench, sitting cross-legged, he turned to face her.

"Dark beauty, light in shadow, what would you have of me?"

"You want several things from *me.*"

He laid out his palm, open.

"At any time, you may release yourself from my service."

"Not without loss."

"But would that loss come from me?"

"No."

"I am the scapegoat. I will take this on if you need me to. It is best if a scapegoating ritual is done consciously."

This wasn't his fault. But she felt closed in on, trapped.

"I know you've already slept with Joanie."

"That was her desire."

"I know you wish I were in your bed too."

He looked at her under his eyebrows.

"I exist greatly in the moment. I am in hundreds of thousands of moments. Of these moments, many are of great value. Mine with you are of great value."

"You need to go back to flirting school, angel."

"O harsh and beautiful one, how shall I flirt with you?"

She let herself smile.

"Gently."

t their coffee shop, Gus and Julia perched at a table outside—metal, painted white, a little wet from last night's rain. Above them, wind shook bud-covered branches, carrying the scent of flowers.

Julia spooned whipped cream off the top of her frappé.

"I'm sure you saw the video on the news," she said.

"How is Odin's Hunt taking it?" Julia had to have gone to Linda for the gossip.

"Apparently Bruni totally freaked out." Bruni had taken the reins after Max left for Europe. "He was never in favor of Max going after your friend. She's just a girl, weak and unimportant." She made a face. "He would have understood if it was you."

"Did the Hunt know about Max's stuff in Europe?"

"Oh yeah. They were in on all that. They did Mark Walker favors sometimes. Beat people up for him, that kind of thing. Mark repaid them—he helped build that hall at Odinshof they're so proud of."

"Now that connection's gone."

"Pretty much. Bruni doesn't have his shit together enough to talk to a rich Austrian widow."

Her eyes met his, hers dark brown, a ring of amber around the pupil.

"If your witch friends' magic did that, they're onto something powerful."

"I don't know how that works. I wasn't part of that."

Julia sipped her drink. "Max's family's coming to pick up the body. Odin's Hunt wants to do a service for him on the land."

She put her hand over his.

"I'm sorry."

"Don't be. The Max I was in love with was gone a long time ago. If he ever existed."

He still missed what had been.

He remembered the first time he kissed Max, in the alley behind the Leviathan, when Max crushed him into the brick wall. He remembered sex like fire and wine.

He remembered, two years ago, climbing a mountain with Max, in the hush of a snowy night, under a waning half moon.

Max had shoved him off that mountain.

Chapter 33

That evening, walking toward Puabi through the twilight, Azazel appeared in his most regal dress, a long, dark-blue, deeply embroidered robe tricked out with gold necklaces, black wings spread and feathers ruffling gently.

She watched him approach with pleasure—her murderous, handsome angel.

But he wasn't hers.

In the cool dusk, waiting for him on the bench at the edge of lamplight, she drew her own black robe tight around her. Somewhere among the tents, someone played a pipe, a haunting melody.

He'd never introduced her to his tribe.

She was only one of hundreds, even thousands of connections for him, not even a lover.

Stepping up to the bench, he raised his eyebrows, and she nodded. The silver wine service appeared, on a low table. She let him fill her cup. He sat, disappearing his wings.

"What next, my fearsome lord?"

"I go to your ladies."

"You think we should go to Inanna as well as Ereshkigal?"

"I do. I think we should visit her first."

"Why? I thought you were friends with Ereshkigal."

"Ereshkigal and I knew each other in passing, in another age of the world. Inanna and I once had an alliance. I hope she will help pave my way into her sister's good graces."

"I'm at least as likely to do that as Inanna is."

A hint of smile crossed his face. "It is good to have as many allies as possible in a campaign."

"True."

"So, my dark beauty, how am I to approach your queen?"

She inclined her head.

"Don't you and Inanna... um... know each other? I would show a little more skin, if I were you. Maybe that red kilt you like."

"My showing skin does not attract you, however."

"Oh, I wouldn't say that. I'm just—" She sighed and rolled her eyes.

"Shy?"

"Annoying."

With a shimmer, he transformed to wearing his long red kilt, obediently enough.

"How does one seduce a succubus?"

"Let her do the seducing."

He slid closer to her, enveloping her in the scent of dark frankincense. A stray black hair tickled her cheek.

"Let me know if at any time you would like to start."

She looked up at him, biting the inside of her cheek, desire flowing upward through her like warm honey.

Her scent rose, and his nostrils flared.

She stood.

"You wanted to see Inanna. But first—you like frankincense, right? She does too. We should bring her some."

Immediately, on the bench, a silver bucket appeared, piled high with brown-gold chunks of frankincense.

"Great. Now to find the lady. But how?"

"To exit this pocket hell, I must be called."

"Well, then, Lord Azazel, I call you to accompany me to visit my goddess Inanna."

In a building across the path from the stand of palms, a door opened. In the doorway showed a sea of stars.

"I follow you, enchantress."

With a few steps, they crossed the path. Through the door, they stepped into a heaven of stars that rolled outward blazing, suns of emerald, gold, ruby, and blue topaz.

Among these on an intricately woven carpet sat a throne, gold inlaid with lapis and carnelian. Before it stood a gilt incense burner, heavy with burning coal. Here, Azazel poured out the frankincense, wings spread behind him.

Almost immediately, Inanna appeared on her throne, in a Sumerian gown of tiered linen and a conical gold crown, her eyes ringed in shadow. Her nipples peaked below the sheer cloth.

She'd never shown up that quickly for Puabi-Ekur.

"Lord Azazel! What an unexpected pleasure! Puabi-Ekur, have you been, um, hanging around with Azazel?"

She wasn't sure how to answer, but Azazel stepped in.

"We remet when her human consort performed ritual for the Watcher angels."

"How nice. What you brings you here?"

"Desire for your lovely presence."

Inanna went a little red.

"And desire for a favor."

"What favor is that?"

"I seek allies to help release my legions—to send them on the next step in their journey."

"That's more my sister's domain."

"My hope is you would help plead my case for me."

Inanna eyed Puabi-Ekur—still in her Puabi form.

"I believe your companion can do this better than I."

He flicked a glance at Puabi.

"Puabi-Ekur is one of Ereshkigal's favored," the goddess said.

"I do not doubt that."

Inanna looked from one of them to the other.

"But you two—"

He shook his head.

"She does not so choose." He threw a sardonic look at Puabi.

Puabi stuck her tongue out at him.

"Oh, I see," said the love goddess, glancing between them. "Then you won't mind if I borrow him for a little." Her eyes sparkled. "Come with me, Lord Azazel of the many talents."

A door opened in the starry expanse, showing beyond it warm light and a filmy golden curtain. From the doorway floated a scent of honey. The goddess led him through by the hand, and the sky shut behind them.

Puabi-Ekur stared.

It would support his cause, but it wasn't what they'd expected.

Puabi-Ekur thought themselves back to their particular lair on the astral, a fluffy bit of cloud in the aether. Azazel was a big boy—he could get himself home.

So frustrated, they were nearly crying.

They had a crush on him, and he was open to it. He had asked them to seduce him.

They hadn't had sex since inhabiting Clayton, through whom they'd met Joanie, which for an incubus-succubus was odd. Though they thought of Joanie as their girlfriend, they weren't having sex with her. They could have asked for that, but they hadn't. They'd retreated into devotions to their deities and work for Hekate.

Were they even an incubus-succubus anymore?

They were changing state, but what that meant they didn't know.

But torturing themselves about someone who'd said in so many words he wanted them—who furthermore knew exactly who they were, as only a spirit can know a spirit— what was the point?

It wasn't sex they were afraid of.

As an incubus-succubus, they'd always been in charge. With a Watcher angel who was their boss, that would not be so.

Yet Azazel had never tried to push them around. In his odd, unflirtatious way, he'd told them they were important to him.

If they were jealous of Azazel going off with Inanna, it

meant they were feeling underappreciated. They hardly needed to. The door was open; they'd been invited inside.

But to enter, to participate, they'd have to let go a little control.

Or else they'd suffer in silence while everyone else had sex with Azazel.

Chapter 34

Saturday morning, Cleo was in the bedroom, considering how best to tack up a ceiling covering. She'd gotten a new one, white with silver sparkles, and a few throw pillows to match, to suit the bright light of the bedroom.

Joanie was watching, ready to lend a hand. But Cleo was the designer.

"How about that?"

"Works for me."

"Let's take a break, then unpack a few more boxes."

In the kitchen, Joanie made espresso on their stovetop machine, in a separate small saucepan heated milk. For home, she contented herself with lattes, but a good espresso maker was on her short list for future purchase.

"I can't get over Max being gone," Cleo said.

Joanie had been keeping Cleo apprised of her talks with the angel. Cleo warily approved of him.

"This way you don't have to shoot anyone."

"I just can't feel he's completely gone."

For the next Sabbat, Oestara, they combined forces with Nora's small coven. Olivia had hived off to form a new group. Jackie and Shaun had gone with her, so now in total Nora's coven held three people.

They drove out on a Sunday, with high billows of cloud on saturated blue. Along the way, birds called, robins after worms in green yards. Early tulips flared from boxes and raised beds—red, violet, yellow. Further out of the city, fir and cedar surrounded them, heads thrown up against the sky.

Joanie drove, Cleo rode shotgun. In back, Gus and Alyssa broke into the cookies, pale shortbread with pink icing. They'd cracked the windows open—spring had come at last. On the air hung the smell of flowers.

At Nora's, they piled out. The big, rambling house smelled of baking. Nora stood in the kitchen, cutting up hard-boiled eggs to devil. Hannah pulled in a few minutes later and gave everyone hugs.

Nora hugged back, but the smile fell off her face quickly. Over the last weeks, two live-in coveners and farm helpers had moved out, leaving only one. One of the greenhouses was boarded up, in need of repair. A tree had collapsed onto it in a winter ice storm.

Was Nora's dream falling apart? Joanie had dreamed of a farm herself, but she didn't know what the bridge was to that from the present.

Olivia, Jackie, and Shaun appeared at the last minute. Olivia came and kissed Nora—her leavetaking had been amicable. Jackie and Shaun hung back, and Joanie got the sense Olivia had dragged them along.

They held the opening circle outdoors, on a green lawn edged by native salal. After Nora and Hannah cut the circle, they trooped to Nora's small cabin, bearing garlands and food-gifts for Dea, the lady of the land.

Quieter among the trees, except for birdsong, the woods made Joanie think of Pete. This was the place where he'd found his connection with the Horned God. Boughs of cedar draped delicate tracery, gave scent when they brushed her face; firs loomed dark and thick, punctuated by pale trunks of alder.

They reached the tiny cedar-shake cabin, its door engraved with an ivy-twined pentacle. A fire in the wood-stove warmed the space.

"Lady, we offer you these gifts." Piece by piece, Nora fed the food offerings to the fire.

They settled, and Nora and Hannah led a meditation. In it, they wandered through the woods to a small glade, where Dea manifested on a woven-wood throne, wearing garlands of daffodils, tulips, and early hyacinth from the greenhouse.

To Joanie, she said, "You have been sad and now are happy. Your beloved Horned God is making his way to the mighty dead and the gods. He loves you still. Do you want to see him?"

"Of course!"

A reddish light glowed in the green haze, and he was there: lanky, pale, red-haired, forked horns rising from his close-cropped hair.

Swimming forward through the mist-edged light, he kissed her.

How often she'd awakened from a dream of his falling, longing for him, blaming herself. Though not lately.

Being a spirit, he could read her mind.

"You know it was never your fault. I chose my path." She let herself take his words in. "I'm happy you have a new companion. I want someone to take care of you."

"Are you happy?"

"Oh, Joanie, I'm learning so much. I miss you, I wish I could be with you, but this time has been amazing. And I owe a lot to Dea." He glanced sideways, to where the statue stood.

They were lovers on the astral, then.

Jealousy flashed through her. She did her best to let it go.

Nora's voice drifted in: "Now say good-bye to the goddess and any spirits who have come to you."

"Good-bye, sweetheart."

"Good-bye. I can't come to you yet in dream or meditation, except for some special time like this. There are things I must finish. But soon."

"Of course." Hannah had said the newly dead needed a couple years to settle in.

She felt it then, how much she missed him. Cleo and she were solid, but busy, their sustaining love often in the background. Azazel amazed her, but he couldn't be with her in the day to day. She'd lost Pete when they were still head-over-heels in hard, wet, physical, human love.

She looked helplessly at Dea, who nodded. At least the goddess was there for him.

"Good-bye, Lady. Thank you."

After that, they dragged a table onto the greensward rising from the creek, threw a lace-edged white cloth over it, and put out their fare: deviled eggs, salads, hothouse fruit, rosemary biscuits. Someone had brought a roast chicken. Hannah passed around prosecco.

While Cleo caught Hannah up on her recent work, Joanie wandered down to the pond, sipping prosecco. Not far along its encircling path stood a wooden bench, fashioned out of hewn logs from the property, and she sat.

Water reflected the blue of the sky. A few frogs croaked. Earlier in the day, they'd seen a heron, but he was gone now.

Stretching in the sunlight, she basked, letting it soak into and relax her.

A finch alighted on a low-hanging alder branch, watched her a moment, and flew off.

She could get used to the peace of this place.

On the way out, she gave Nora a hug, Cleo standing beside them.

"You're looking for apprentices and live-in help."

"I am."

"Unfortunately, we just took a year lease."

Nora met Joanie's eyes. Hers were a clear green-brown, like the water of a brook with a mossy bottom.

"Maybe that's a blessing in disguise. I've had people move in and had it not work. That's considerably more painful than getting to know each other slowly. In the meantime, any time you want to get out into the countryside or help with the farm work, I'm open. I just need a day or so notice."

"I might take you up on that. I'm finishing some classes, but I think I'm going to take the summer off school." She'd been driving herself hard for several years. She needed to catch her breath.

"I might too," said Cleo. "I'm doing ancestral work. My ancestors have been telling me they were farmers."

Chapter 35

After greeting Dea at the ritual, Puabi-Ekur returned to their cloud high in the aether.

They were still frustrated, mostly with themselves. They were making something hard that could be easy. It was just that they knew this wouldn't be one and done, as for centuries they'd preferred.

They trusted Azazel with Joanie, who in many ways was more important to them than their own being. Azazel had killed for Joanie.

Inanna trusted Azazel. Also, anyone who could make a sex goddess blush had to have something going on.

Why exactly had Hekate subcontracted their work to Azazel? He was someone who'd drag them into life despite themself; they'd seen that already.

Azazel had handed them the keys to this seduction, if they wanted them.

As Puabi, she chose her weapons. A diaphanous dusty-pink gown, high-waisted, with a golden belt. Gold hoop earrings, a gold pendant of an exquisitely detailed rose. Makeup, discreet yet obvious—she put on a little more kohl than the angel wore himself. Lipstick a shade darker than the dress. A perfume with an overlay of rose and an underlay of musk.

The accouterments were easy.

Apparently, from their fear and excitement, this was what they wanted more than anything right now. There could hardly be an easier seduction—all they had to do was tip their hand.

But, having not been expected, Puabi sat on the bench a long time.

Wind soughed in the palm leaves; night passed. A hint of dawn ringed the space and became evening again, as if the chariot of the sun had circled just below the horizon. She swam in and out of consciousness—not cold, not hot, not anything. She'd materialized a light wrap against the breeze.

It didn't feel right, this time, to find the chasm and bring him water.

She sat propped against the palm trunk, spiny bark poking her back, half-asleep, when a shadow fell across her.

He squatted down, tilted his head gazing at her.

"My dark flower, have you been waiting long?"

"What—oh. Hi. A little while."

"I am sorry to make you wait. Especially as you dressed up for me."

He wore a dark-red robe, little embroidery, little adornment, only his golden sigil necklace. The contrast embarrassed her.

He sat down next to her.

Even the loose robe showed his warrior's hard-muscled arms and legs. His long black hair fell in waves, curling at the ends. Dawn light burnished his brown skin and voluptuous lips, touched his pale grey-blue eyes outlined in kohl.

The pink sky brought out the rose color of her dress.

"Pretty," he said, stroking the skirt along her thigh. "Clearly, you did not plan to wait so long. But you had some intent?"

She yawned. "You're going to wonder how I ever get my job done."

"I see a spirit in the middle of great change. I myself have gone through great change, over time."

"You are kind to me."

He raised an eyebrow. "Am I?"

Rosy light reflecting off the sand lit his eyes lavender.

She put her lips to his, the barest touch.

"Puabi-Ekur! Azazel!"

Azazel let out a grunt of frustration.

Chapter 36

Things had started getting weird in the new apartment.

One night, all the lights shut off together with a sizzle, then turned back on.

The next night, the lights flickered, on-off, on-off, on-off, strobing, nearly a minute, then stopped. Cleo was at her desk, squeezed into a corner of the bedroom, following up work email. Joanie was in her office doing homework.

She crossed to prop herself in the bedroom doorway.

"Cleo, have you noticed weird shit around here lately?"

"You mean like the lights just now?"

"And last night. Also I've fallen a couple of times on the steps—it's like they're booby-trapped."

"Last week, yeah. I was worried."

The half-flight up from the parking lot had been slick with black ice that frosty late-March morning. On her way out in the morning, Joanie fell.

She stood up again quickly, clamped to the wrought-iron

railing, but when she released it she fell again. She hit her head so hard on the step behind that it knocked her out.

On waking, her head spun. She saw sparkles of light.

Now they looked at each other.

All of these were from the spirit bag of tricks.

"There's someone on the spirit plane who's mad at us," Joanie said.

"You think? Someone who just got whacked?"

With a pop, all the lights went out.

Joanie turned on the flashlight on her phone. Cleo found a lighter and lit a couple candles on the windowsill.

The maintenance guy showed up within a half-hour—he lived in the complex. He was in his late forties, gruff and grey-stubbled. They followed him to the garage, where he unlocked and poked at their breaker box. All the breakers were off. He flipped them back on, and the lights returned—no noise, no explosion.

"Did you turn on anything new, anything that would cause a strain on the system?"

"No."

"I don't know what would have done it otherwise."

He looked from one to the other, then shrugged.

"Let me know if it happens again." The place probably wasn't wired to code.

They went to bed.

A rumble and crash woke them in the middle of the night. Things hurtled to the bed and floor with clatters and thumps.

"Ow!"

Their new bookcase had fallen to a 45-degree lean, dropping their books, a granite mortar and pestle, Cleo's boxed stockpile of rocks and bones, and Joanie's collection of glass animals.

"Are you okay?" Cleo asked.

Joanie gasped.

"Look."

Above their heads, toward the ceiling, rocks, bones, and glass spun in circles, lit by blue-white light.

Cleo sat up and stared—then threw herself down again before a flying geode hit her head.

"Puabi-Ekur! Azazel!"

Chapter 37

Immediately they were both in armor, Azazel winged, Puabi-Ekur in male form, heading toward the voice.

They stopped above the bedroom, a half-step away on the astral.

Above Joanie's and Cleo's bed, a contingent of warrior djinn flew circling in the air, screaming and laughing. Leading them, one burly, scarlet-horned one looked like Max.

Puabi-Ekur had identified Max long ago as a djinni in human form. Djinn had a particular type of insanity—they thought of themselves as gods, as Max had. As Max did.

"What should we do?"

"I must rally my company. But before that, I must introduce you. It is only courtesy."

Fear clutched Ekur's throat. It didn't feel right to leave, though they could return instantly from the Earth-plane point of view. He fought it down.

"Um, okay. That makes sense."

They landed at the oasis, both still in armor. Red sunset dyed the edge of the sky. Azazel unfurled his wings behind him, a thundercloud of black.

Ekur cut his eyes toward the black tents.

"Do you have wives or companions among your company?"

"I do not. A few occasional lovers among my men, but not for centuries. You need fear no jealousy there."

The corner of his lip lifted in a smile.

"How should I introduce you? I wish for us to continue your experiment."

"Would you introduce me differently if I were your lover?"

"I might not use different words."

His men, Watcher angels, and their human families had all gone into exile with him millennia ago. They knew him well enough to understand him without words.

"They would respect anyone beside whom I stood."

But spirits, especially the fallen, had a fine-grained sense of rank. A companion would have a higher rank.

All in armor, in male form, Ekur was still half a head shorter. He had to stand on tiptoe for a kiss.

"Consider that a promise."

"Come with me, then."

Dawn had passed, and daylight was a pale band along the horizon in this twilit world.

The scent of woodsmoke met them among the black tents.

The shadows lay darker there. Ghostly forms passed; light glimmered off breastplates.

Beyond, a fire burned, sparks fizzing upward from it. Azazel stepped up to the flames, which burned higher, responding to the wind around him.

"My warrior chieftains, I would like to introduce a new companion, Puabi-Ekur. We have been called to fight a band of djinn, and Puabi-Ekur is going to fight with us."

A rustling in the silence, and a voice called out, "Greetings, Puabi-Ekur."

Another few voices said, "Greetings."

"Arm yourselves, gather your legions, and Puabi-Ekur will lead us to the battle."

The company scattered, made ready, with the clank of soldiers grabbing spears, the click of breastplates being fastened. As angels returned, they moved into the firelight, and the shadows became more clear: many hundred warriors, mostly men, a few women among them.

"Lead," Azazel said to Puabi. "I will open the doorway."

Into a shadowy fog, they went, through to the room where books, rocks, and glass animals spun, gleaming blue-white light. The angels surrounded the room, partly in and partly out of the astral.

"Puabi-Ekur, take these two soldiers, and protect the young women as they leave the room."

Two angels followed Ekur, all three putting their shields above them, crawling toward the bed. Ekur crept up and whispered in Joanie's ear.

"Let's get you two out of the room while Azazel and his company fight the djinn."

They slipped out of the bed and clambered along the floor.

Above them, above the circling objects, swords rang,

engaging. The ceiling had become a puff of thundercloud against twilight dark-blue, twelve feet up, twenty feet up, further. The corners of the room reappeared as the clouds thinned, then disappeared again, as if one reality overlaid the other.

Blue-white lights flashed in a cloud of turbulence. Pale light shone along a sword, another, glittered on chain mail, struck pink against the djinn's skin, dark-red.

Out of the bedroom, they closed the door.

"I'd suggest warding it. I'm going to go fight."

Back in the room, dozens of separate fights tumbled, lights striking like lightning hidden in cloud. Angels' swords, maces, spears countered the djinn's in a twilight sky. The djinn floated like smoke—they favored long knives, shoved up under the angel's armor. Flyers hit one another and ricocheted away. The djinn laughed, hooting, as they fought. The fallen angels' faces were grim. One by one, the djinn winked out, to another plane. The last few, including Max, fought a rear-guard action.

Throwing himself forward, Ekur slashed at Max.

He parried. He and another djinni backed away, swords flashing. Then these last two winked out of the material plane and were gone.

The last few floating objects dropped to bed and floor with bangs and thumps.

The rest of the angelic company disappeared, leaving only Ekur and Azazel, hovering in the air above the rumpled bed.

"Now what?" Ekur asked.

"We should make sure they ward carefully. And check in

more often. The djinn are gone for now, but they will return."

"How can we get rid of them for good?"

"I had thought Max an ordinary man. If he is a djinni, the concerns are different."

"That's my understanding—he's a djinni who lived as a mortal man."

"I wish I had known this, incubus."

Hadn't he known to look?

"Are they different to fight?"

"As a djinni, he is now released from mortal constraints. The strategy is war—fight and keep fighting until they understand they cannot win."

"Very well." It sounded exhausting. They'd take one step at a time. "I'll tell Joanie and Cleo they can have their room back."

Joanie paused in the doorway, yawning. The bed was a mess of books, rocks, and glass creatures.

"We need at least to get the stuff off the bed."

Rolling her shoulders, Cleo went into the bedroom and started shelving.

"Max and his friends will probably be back," Puabi-Ekur said. "Ward well, and I'll make sure there's a spirit protecting the perimeter. Me, or Azazel, or one of his company."

"I can't believe he's dead and I still have to deal with him."

They had spent so much energy on him, so much fear and reaction, so many plans, only to have him return. Somewhere inside her lurked mind-numbing fear, but mostly right now exhaustion.

Fucking djinn.

"We'll figure it out."

Angel and incubus both kissed her cheek, slid ecto-plasmic arms around her in an embrace, then disappeared.

Chapter 38

*B*ack at the oasis, Azazel leaped onto a rock by the legion tents. Firelight lit him from below, shining against his bronze breastplate.

"Good work, my warriors! I shall get you your reward soon."

He dispatched a guard to look after Joanie. The rest of the company returned to their tents—a few wounded, none badly.

To Ekur, Azazel said, "Come talk to me in my tent."

Still in armor, Ekur followed the angel.

Darkness was falling. A sandy path lined with flickering torches led away from the black tents. They took it, Azazel tucking away his wings. Picking up Ekur's hand, he raised it to his lips and kissed it.

"I had not seen you fight before, Puabi-Ekur."

"You saw very little that time. I was scrambling to get a stroke in."

"I know little about you."

"We know little about each other."

"You know my legend. I would like to hear the story of Puabi-Ekur."

The angel's pavilion mounted black against blue twilight. They pushed though the door.

Inside, candles blazed. On the near side of a bed dressed in black silk sat a low couch and gilt-edged ebony table. On this sat the silver wine service.

Puabi-Ekur wanted to change out of their armor. It was tempting to change back to Puabi—that tugged at them.

But what form was most truly theirs?

Female? Male? Something of both? A wraith with no gendered features at all?

"Like yours, my story is long. I can tell the highlights if you like. But if we were human, I'd pull off my armor and settle into a bath, if I could."

"A bath sounds delightful."

Across the space from couch and table appeared a large wooden tub, filled with steaming hot water. Rose petals floated on it, scent threading the air. Beside it sat a wooden bench, a couple of towels folded over it.

Azazel wanted their story. If they went back to the beginning, their first form was of Puabi, dancer of Uruk. They transformed to her, hair pinned up for the bath, attired in a bath towel. Dropping that, she climbed in.

Divested of wings and clothes, Azazel followed.

Twilight fell to darkness. The candles blazed, none burning out. The bathwater stayed hot.

"Do you miss it, traveling, with no connection to the mortal world except by choice?"

"Sometimes. But I re-engaged for a reason, and I took up service. I could not go back now and be the same."

"I understand."

She took his right hand—a broad brown palm, a scar at its heel, rings on several fingers. One was gold, with ancient writing nearly worn away; another was inset with a broad black stone. Around his thumb lay a circlet of silver inlaid with gold writing in another script, also very worn.

"That's Arabic, but I can't quite read it. What does it say?"

"It is a protective charm."

"Does it work?"

"Perhaps somewhat. I was given it as a gift, so I keep it."

She imagined this gift—who knew how long ago.

She kissed his palm.

"How many lovers have you had, since you became incarnate?" she asked. Since lovers was one of the things he'd showed up here for.

"Since the beginning? Thousands. You know I can go into and out of time. Also, we commanders of the Watchers began as seraphim. We have a particular nature. I am not simply one; I am many. I could be here with you, and chained in the chasm, and making love to another far away."

"And are you, right now?"

"Perhaps. I could ask you also—how many lovers have you had?"

"Thousands as well."

Holding his hand in both hers, she kissed his palm again, licked the web of his thumb.

Pulling her toward him, he drew her to lie beside him in

the bath. He settled her head on his nearly dry shoulder, stroked her hair. A few strands dangled into the water.

Slowly, over the bath, over the telling of her story, she'd relaxed. Water clouded with a haze of steam and drifted with rose petals showed their bodies, brown limbs twining.

"And now what, o most beautiful?"

She could come to him either as a woman or a man—if she so desired, as a wind or a shower of rain.

"Let us start from the beginning. Before I was a man, before I was a bodiless spirit, I was a woman. Let us be together as a woman and a man."

She stood up, in all her naked glory, sleek brown body dripping.

He stood, making the bath water bow and wave, cock already at half-mast. She took it in her hand at the base, and on her tiptoes kissed him deeply.

Fire. Angels were made of fire.

He picked her up and lifted her out of the bath, heading for the bed.

"Let me dry off!"

With a grunt, he set her down. She grabbed a towel and rubbed it across herself. Watching him watch her, she slowed, seeing as if through his eyes the contrast of fluffy white on brown skin and dark nipples.

His grey-blue eyes had gone black with pupil. "Now, may I?"

"I'm tempted—" Releasing the towel, she dropped to her knees, licked the head of his cock.

His hand bunched in her hair, then slid downward to catch her under the armpit. He pulled her up.

"No. I have waited a long time. Let me have what I most desire."

He carried her to the wide bed covered with black silk. Above it, candles flickered on gold.

Gently, he laid her down, cupping her breasts a moment with his hands, nuzzling her neck. Then, sliding down, he nudged her onto her back. His tongue trailed along her thigh, circling inward. She trembled to tongue and teeth against her clit, almost too much sensation. The touch unlocked wave after wave, rising into the sea of flame, releasing her once more.

Then, she poised above him, rising and falling, the muscles within her stroking him, watching his face till he filled her, wet and hot. She let herself go again, resonances lighter but sweet, then settled herself to lie beside him. The smell of sweat mixed with rose and frankincense.

Though spirits didn't need to sleep, they slept.

Chapter 39

hen they woke, they held a war council, curled in robes on the couch in his tent. His was dark blue, hers black with a touch of gilt. It made her look like one of the tent's fixtures, but she didn't mind.

He'd snuffed a few candles so they could sleep, reaching out with wind, and what remained was drowsy half-light. On the ebony table sat a silver teapot and tiny cups of hot mint tea.

"We have to get rid of Max and his folk. Or at least persuade them they need to leave Joanie alone."

"I agree. Joanie will never be of full will and heart in this project until her fear is laid to rest."

"Also I'm not sure we should let go a lot of warriors just yet. I mean, the easiest way to get rid of those folks is over-whelming force."

"Yes." He threw himself backward, head hanging back, arm along the back of the couch. "Truly I weary of these conflicts."

She drew her hand down his neck and chest, letting her fingers hang in the neck of his robe. "I want a thousand years just to make love to you."

He half-smiled, a sardonic look, but also she thought more—a little frightening.

"However. You are the angel of swords and knives and shields and coats of mail. So what do we do?"

"Simply fighting him, even winning a battle, will signify nothing unless we beat him soundly."

They needed the type of clear victory that would show they'd always win. Djinn were as immortal as any spirits, but could feel pain, be overpowered and caught.

"What if we trapped him somewhere?"

"When the Watchers were punished, I was locked into Dudael. It is a hell for myself and my company. It is not mine to keep others in."

"I know someone who has her own hell, though. Someone I meant to introduce you to anyway." She tapped her fingers on her lips. "I have an idea. I think we need a note from Inanna."

"What is she going to say?"

"It needs to hint she thinks very highly of you, in a particular way."

He raised an eyebrow. "Are you sure this is the angle at which to approach the Queen of Hell?"

"It worked for me. We have to give her something. We're asking too much not to. When you talked to Inanna, did you explain what you were after?"

"I did."

"Those are the next steps, then. If you're up for that."

"In the legends of the Watchers, it is said that we sampled all things. No act was too extreme."

"Fornication a specialty."

"Exactly, o garden of delight. Summon me to the throne of our lady."

"I need to do something first. You interrupted me."

She slid off the couch. Between his legs, she knelt like a penitent before a god, folding his robe up to his waist.

He stroked her hair, looking down at her.

"Let me do this."

"I cannot promise that I will let you finish."

"Challenge accepted."

His strong thighs with their scrim of hair had a scent of frankincense and musk. His cock was magnificent, thick and long, a test to her abilities, but she was up to it.

He threw back his head and groaned.

Jeweled stars glittered above a throne of gold inlaid with lapis, carnelian, and crystal. To their proposal she write to her sister, Inanna nodded so hard she almost toppled her conical crown.

"I know just the thing."

Clapping her hands, she called two devotees, who brought a clay tablet and a stylus. Looking into the starry sky, she chewed the stylus a moment, then started writing.

"It might be a bit derivative, but my sister will know the form."

Curious, Puabi-Ekur, presenting as Puabi, stood.

"May I see, my lady?" She looked over her shoulder. "Vigorously sprouting? Loins like honey?"

"This is the language of devotional poetry, Puabi-Ekur."

Moving to stand behind Inanna's throne, Azazel smirked.

"I mean, it's not like you're overselling him."

Inanna laughed.

"You shared his bed finally. I was surprised you'd wait."

Puabi's and Azazel's eyes met.

"I believe Puabi-Ekur likes to savor their anticipation, my lady."

"I think the red kilt again."

"You enjoy that outfit. I shall wear it more often."

"I'll just take it off you."

"Empty promises."

"You'll lose it on the way anyway." Ereshkigal's gatekeeper held to the traditional no-clothes-on-entrance rule.

Encircled in his arm, she lay with her head on his shoulder, above her the pavilion ceiling's rippled black silk. Outside of linear time, they'd been in bed for most of a week. Mostly they'd been male and female, though she'd let him take her as a young man. He hadn't let her penetrate him, and she hadn't pushed that. Like anyone trapped, he needed choice. Part of him was always chained to a wall of red-black basalt.

"I do have other plans afoot, should this approach not be successful or sufficient. I will not burden you with details, but if this does not suit, all is not lost."

"You're so mysterious."

"You shall know all soon enough."

"Anyway, we should get moving."

Reaching over, he licked her neck—slowly, taking his time. Then dipped to bite her nipple. She gasped.

"After we speak to the Lady Ereshkigal, we will be busy. However much I would like to halt fighting and bend you over a cloud, I do not think that will be easy."

"I'd be okay with that. I like fucking better than fighting."

"Suspend the fight in time for an orgasm or two?"

"Sure."

"Your wish is my command. Perhaps now."

His fingers found her pussy—a long, slow stroke, another.

He slipped down, and his mouth followed his hand.

Chapter 40

The basalt staircase spiraled downward, carved through living rock, every few yards lit by inset lanterns. The first few were ornate; further on, they were fired clay, then hunks of rock each holding a puddle of burning oil. Then the only light was a faint red glow from below.

Puabi-Ekur traveled as Puabi. Azazel wore his wings, a foot higher than his head but folded in close, stray black feathers fluttering. At each gate, she and Azazel left clothing and jewelry.

By the final gate, basalt bound with silver, they stood stripped nude. At the gatekeeper's gesture, Azazel left his last jewelry, his warded ring, on a plinth of hewn rock.

His eyes lingered on it a moment.

"You'll get it back," Puabi whispered.

Now they carried only Inanna's tablet of poetry, wrapped in undyed linen in a gilded wooden box.

"It is a gift to the Lady Ereshkigal from her sister," Puabi told the gatekeeper, who let them keep it.

The final gate, silver gleaming red, opened before them without sound. Torches flared on either side. The gatekeeper disappeared, and they stood alone in the vast forecourt of the Great Below, walls receding into black, the floor dust on stone.

A deep, booming voice from one side of the space said, "To what do I owe the pleasure, Puabi-Ekur? And who is your companion?"

On a giant throne of basalt, inset with black chalcedony, sat a black-robed form. Skin stretched thin over a skull with deep-set eyes, red irises holding horizontal black pupils like a goat's.

Azazel showed no distress—he was used to the denizens of hell.

Puabi stepped up to the base of the throne. The red light intensified. "Hail, Lady of the Great Below, Queen of the Dead."

Azazel echoed her, and they laid themselves prone in obeisance.

"You may rise."

They stood. The lady had shifted aspect, her face now a Sumerian queen's, framed in crimped black hair, still with uncanny red eyes.

"This is Lord Azazel, who may be known to you," Puabi said. "He is one of the Watcher angels, early upon the Earth."

Azazel bowed his head. His skin glowed in the red light, his wings a moving cloud behind him, shading into darkness. No gatekeeper could take those, or his warrior's muscles, or his face cut like an idol's.

"We have a gift for you, great lady, from your sister."

"You may come forward."

Puabi laid the box in her lady's lap. Ereshkigal untied and opened it.

"She sent me poetry!"

Puabi cleared her throat. "My lady, we are petitioners here, in two ways. So let our gifts to you be generous."

Ereshkigal looked up from the tablet, red eyes sparkling.

"You come to me naked. The only gift I see is poetry from my sister."

"My lady, I came to you naked on other days, yet you found my gifts to you pleasing."

"Truly your gifts have been jewels beyond price." The goddess looked the angel up and down. "Even naked, the Lord Azazel could be called a gift."

"My lady." His deep voice rumbled in the cavelike black room. "Let whatever humble offering I can make be yours."

"Such generosity," she said, with an unearthly grin, her teeth long yellow fangs. "What do you desire?"

"My lady, we have two requests. One has to do with the fate of a particular dead man."

Her nose wrinkled. "You may offer food and beer for your dead, but do not seek their release."

"That's not what we want, my lady. Quite the opposite. My beloved Joanie has been harassed for months by an evil man. He has stalked her, threatened her, and tried to kill her. Then Lord Azazel killed him. Yet this man did not descend to hell, but rather became a part of a troop of djinn who still harass her."

"Unfortunate, though not unusual."

"We can protect her, my lady," Azazel said. "But we

would make her protection complete."

"My lady, since he was a man till just days ago, can he not be held in the Great Below?"

The goddess stroked her cheekbone with a long, bony finger.

"If he died as a man, he is subject to men's afterlife. But you can't expect my galla demons to go after him."

"My lady, we will secure him, if you will cage him."

"And what will I get in return?"

Puabi gestured with a sweep of her hand. "All we can offer."

Ereshkigal smirked.

"Very well. Consider that wish granted. Though capturing a djinni is no easy task, for all the stories about bottles and lamps. You said you had a second request."

Azazel took a step forward.

"O dread lady, you may know the story of the Watcher angels."

"If I did, I have forgotten it."

"We came to Earth to teach the people and make love to them."

"A worthy goal."

"But not to the liking of Yaldabaoth."

The goddess hissed. "Say not the name of the Usurper here!"

Puabi and Azazel traded a glance.

"We're not fans either, my lady. That's our point."

"He created a prison for myself and my angel company. I do not seek release; I incited rebellion. But my people followed me for love. It has been millennia, and I would free those who wish to go on."

He paced forward and dropped to one knee.

"I believe you can give them that gift, my lady. I ask it as a boon."

Her red eyes shone.

"I have tools of special sanction. But it is customary to give such things to a human devotee."

"We're aware of that, my lady. We've asked my beloved Joanie to help us. We merely wished to find if it were possible."

"It is."

From the basalt throne, inset black chalcedony shone dully, reflecting red light.

"My sister's poetry is persuasive. You offer services similar to Puabi-Ekur's, Lord Azazel?"

"My lady, I do. To secure your support, I would do much."

"Very well. My servant shall show you both to a chamber in my palace, Ganzir."

She disappeared. A tall man in a tiered Sumerian robe and a long, oiled grey beard advanced.

"Follow me."

Amid dust, silence, and the whispers of the dead, shades passed them. Some lingered to watch them go by. In the distance, jewel tones glowed from a walled garden. Most was chilly blue-black darkness, except for their guide's lantern, glowing gold.

Puabi let herself fall back a step.

"Are you really up for this?"

"Have faith in a fallen angel, Puabi-Ekur."

"It's the rising part I'm concerned about." Ereshkigal was

capable of appearing in skeletal form, according to her whim.

"When we are alone, I shall tell you a few stories. In the meantime, trust me."

Their guide glanced back, and she shut her mouth.

Hundreds of steps ascended along a ramp to a pair of massive pillars of polished basalt. At the top, they turned to walk down a long hallway, flanked by mosaics in lapis lazuli and dark red stone. Above the scent of dust hovered the oily smell of lantern smoke.

They continued to a door whose basalt frame was inlaid with colored mosaic. In a frieze along the header, the Lady received tribute. The servant opened the door and gestured them through.

Azazel glamoured his wings away. The servant shut the door behind them.

They faced a vast bed, its frame carven wood inlaid with gold and silver, covered with a tawny fur coverlet thrown back to show black smoothly shining sheets. From black ceramic braziers to either side wafted cypress and juniper smoke.

A side door opened, and the goddess reappeared as a Sumerian queen, in a draped gown of gossamer-thin white linen. Her eyes no longer glowed red, but were dark-brown, ringed with kohl.

She climbed upon the bed, and pulling out a few embroidered pillows propped herself against them. "Come, join me."

They did. From a far room floated a flute-song. The Lady smelled of cedar oil.

Puabi scooted forward, kissing the goddess's cheek.

Azazel sat leaning to one side; from the other side, Puabi beckoned him near.

"We shall serve you as you best desire, my lady."

The linen gown disappeared.

Puabi met Azazel's eyes. He blinked, watching her closely.

Kissing her way down from the Lady's cheek, she lightly kissed and licked the Lady's nipple. She glanced up at Azazel, who understood and mirrored her.

They gently smoothed and kissed the brown body, stroked the smooth skin. Ereshkigal sighed and gasped. The scent of cedar oil rose as Azazel lipped and bit one nipple as Puabi laved the other.

They massaged her vulva. Puabi licked as Azazel— glancing for permission—pushed fingers inside. The Lady gasped and groaned.

"More!"

"What is it you desire, my lady?"

She looked at Azazel under her eyelashes.

"Beautiful goddess," he said, "to worship you is a gift beyond my best dreams."

They shifted, and Puabi took the top of her body, her long hair brushing over her. "You like that?" she whispered. "You like that?"

Azazel leaned over her body, licking her in long strokes, his fingers inside her. She wriggled, asking for more.

With a few strokes of his hand, he was fully hard. He teased her with his cock, nudging her. "Do you want this?"

"Yes!"

Slow, teasing, he entered and pulled out. Then shoved in. The goddess gasped. Puabi kissed and licked her nipples.

They fell back against the pillows, panting. The sweet smell of sex mixed with a tang of sweat, a hint of cedar oil from the Lady.

A light drum and lyre had joined the music of the flute. Ereshkigal rang a bell, and servants brought a flagon of beer and some dates on silver plates with gilt overlaid in designs. In the Sumerian afterlife, the dead ate and drank, and so did their mistress.

"That was lovely," said the Lady, stretching. "You both should stay a while."

"What about your husband—Lord Nergal?" Puabi asked. Legend said they'd married after Ereshkigal had him dragged back to the Great Below because she missed him, and when he returned they'd had sex for six days.

Ereshkigal waved her hand vaguely.

"Nergal has his concubines."

"You two aren't on good terms?"

"We're not on bad terms. We've been married literally for millennia. We allow each other our freedom. He would be concerned if my lovers started offering judgment on the dead, or something equally presumptuous. But that I have one or two paramours? Not a concern."

She grinned toothily.

"Don't worry about the God of Plagues. Maybe rest a little and begin again?"

"Of course, my lady," said the angel.

On the staircase up from the Great Below, at each gate they received back jewelry and clothing. Azazel slipped on his thumb ring scribed with Arabic, rubbing it.

At the oasis, dawn paled the sky, an empty color like water. It reflected in his eyes.

"Come back to my tent with me, Puabi-Ekur."

Still Puabi, she nodded wordlessly. He took her hand, kissed her knuckles.

"You are pensive, star of heaven."

"We've gotten the initial agreement. But, as they say, our work is cut out for us."

"Have confidence, most beautiful. We pair well together, for seduction and for battle."

They walked down the center of the line of torches toward the pavilion. Each winked out as they passed. Candles in the gilt candelabra lit themselves as they entered the tent.

"We should check in on Joanie."

"I trust my men to have looked out for her."

Joanie was in good hands, and they both needed a rest.

Climbing onto the gilt bed covered with black silk, Puabi pulled off her long earrings and set them on the ebony bed-table.

"We seem to be spending a lot of time in bed."

"All too soon we will raise the sword again, Puabi-Ekur."

"Speaking of which…" She slipped her hand into his kilt.

They'd made a gift of pleasure to the Queen of the Great Below. Now they closed the space around themselves, only for them two.

His hand stroked her long hair; she met his kiss. Love fluttered and banked like flame.

Chapter 41

The silver tray set amid the black silk sheets, Azazel poured Puabi a cup of wine.

"I have a concern. Over time, a number of your human paramours have come to the attention of the djinn-folk."

"Yes, if the number is two."

"Saadiya, our mutual beloved, is clearly on their list."

"Her first attacker, her sugar daddy, Phil—I don't know if he has any connection to this later bunch. Max showed up because of Gus originally. Then he happened to know the man that Pete the Horned God killed."

"You do not think she has drawn a djinn king's notice? That would be a danger."

Ever since Puabi-Ekur had been with Joanie, djinn had showed up to mess with her. But they hadn't sensed a djinn king.

"I don't think the sugar daddy has anything to do with Max. I think Joanie's just shiny. Once as a human you're visible to the unseen world, you stay visible. For Max, I think, she's unfinished business."

"If so, our plan should work. If there is further interest in her elsewhere, we might have to call in allies."

Puabi laughed.

"We've got allies. We did a lot to have allies. Maybe we can set up a going rate, like an orgasm per galla demon or something."

"Dress, and we can research how to perform this plan."

She made a face. "You want me to wear clothes? You ask a lot, angel."

The angel raised an eyebrow. "Recall this is a shared hell. Winds full of sand and grit come up, not of my devising."

She thought of him chained against the wall and kept her mouth shut.

Azazel stored his library of magical books in a cave hollowed in the side of the chasm, with a narrow goat-path down. He carried her there, flying in his arms, though she could have drifted down herself. She didn't mind. From one of the shelves inset into dusty reddish black basalt, he drew a book bound in scuffed brown leather, clasped with an iron binding.

On a small table, he lit a candle, opened the book, and found a page. She followed his finger. She hadn't read Coptic script for centuries, and the text had elisions and torn pages, so it took a while to parse it.

"Capture him and trap him in a lead box. That should work."

"The question would be how to entice him. I fear we shall have to use Saadiya as bait."

"She won't like it, but she'll get it."

A corner of his mouth lifted.

"Perhaps we can persuade her as we persuaded the goddess."

Puabi's jealousy flared—the angel was sleeping with Joanie, and she wasn't. Which meant, perhaps, she should broach that subject with Joanie.

And yet, she couldn't help smiling to herself.

"It's true—she has been dragging her feet in returning to her calling. I mean, as her spiritual guide and her protector, the two of us together must show her the path."

"As teachers, we must demonstrate."

"Exactly."

He shut the book. "I told you I had additional plans. Whether or not this tool we plan obtaining can free my legions, I must pursue these plans. Would you be willing to help?"

She sidled close, stroking his muscled arm.

"Your wish is my command."

He rolled his eyes. "I do not even desire that to be true. But this should be light work. Would you accompany me to a party?"

"I thought you had to be summoned?"

"I was! How can you think no one would invite me to a party?"

"What kind of party?"

"You ask too many questions, succubus. I promise you will come to no harm there."

Pastel irises and crocuses filled the terracotta planters, all blooming at once. Waterlilies pink and gold overflowed from marble fountains; ivy draped painted plaques. Here, the desert pocket realm had been turned into a garden.

Beings scattered across it, some half-there, some very present. Many were angels. Some other diaphanous ones floated, green and some with leaves, nature spirits. Across a wide area, loose groups had formed. Appraising glances followed Puabi, beside Azazel, whose wings were unfurled.

"Come meet my brother," Azazel said to her.

He led her to an arbor, a grapevine over a trellis dripping blue-black grapes with a dusty sheen. Here an angel held court, a being both like and unlike Azazel—more obvious in their genderfluid nature, more splashy in their colors.

In their long, curly hair, threads of purple and dark green mixed with black; their skin had a slight green tinge to its dark brown. Around them gathered a coterie of nature spirits and angels.

"Samyaza!"

"Azazel!"

They embraced each other.

"Who is this?"

Azazel put his hand on Puabi's shoulder, drew her forward.

"Puabi-Ekur." She let her face change subtly, to show Ekur, then shifted back.

"Incubus-succubus?" She nodded. "Definitely good at a party."

Azazel drew her under his arm protectively.

"Puabi-Ekur has been working with me, and we have past experiences together."

"Well met, Puabi-Ekur. Both of you, have a look around!" In a lower voice, to Azazel, Samyaza said, "One of my people will find you."

Someone approached to talk to Samyaza, and Azazel led Puabi away by the elbow.

"What was that about?"

He walked her across the garden, toward the far wall.

"Sam is the ruler of root-cutting—in other words, all pharmakae good and ill. They also make very good cocktails and potions, of various potent forms. Some of their maker folk are even better than they are."

"I'd like not to be altered."

"Alteration is not necessary."

They stopped at a table of decoctions. Azazel gestured to a steaming pot, just set down by one of the green-tinged ones. "That is likely jasmine tea."

Puabi sniffed at it. "I think so." Picking up one of the pretty lavender-and-green mugs, she poured for herself.

"Come see the flame trees in flower."

He led Puabi to trees whose crowns opened to flaring scarlet flowers, amid pale sword-grasses. They stood by the enclosing wall at the space's edge.

Once Azazel and Puabi were well out of earshot of other guests, she raised an eyebrow.

"It is a party, Watchers style. Sam likes parties and spans various worlds. But it is also a conversation."

"How does he do this? I thought you were all locked in separate hells."

"Sam has different affordances because he repented. He

lets us borrow his summoners. But we Watchers must be discreet. The Demiurge ignores an occasional party, but we would all be locked down if he knew we were plotting."

"Plotting about...?"

"When the Demiurge broke the Watchers, it was because his angels incited civil war among us. Now, Sam and I have nearly reunited our Watcher siblings. It has taken work, but it is very close."

"As a backup for what we're doing?"

"Necessary regardless. I do not wish only to free my people."

Azazel looked further, over her shoulder.

A breeze moved around him, circling him, shifting his hair. His own breeze, she sensed, one he'd created.

"What is it?"

Azazel cut his stare. Again taking her arm, he moved to another stand of flame trees, from which arose a green, newly watered scent. Foliage screened them from the party. He nodded toward one of the groups they faced.

"That pale one, very tall?"

"Yes?" She glanced over to a tall, wispy angel, androgynous, with huge silver-grey eyes in a narrow, high-cheekboned face.

"I need to know who brought them, because that person is a traitor. Or has taken forgiveness too far."

"Not your favorite angel?"

"I cannot think of one I like or trust less."

"Who are they?"

"Suriyel, angel of the waning moon. Sometimes they go by Moonshadow. They were with us early, then left to join the Demiurge, laughing at us from the height of the sky. Do not trust them."

They continued to mingle, avoiding the silver-eyed angel. After a time, the party thinned to a number of clumps, each centered around a Watcher. One fiery group needed to stay away from dry plants; another group traveled under a thundercloud; another glittered in colors of the rainbow. Azazel collected a number around himself, friends from when the legions fought together.

At a pause, when he stood alone again with Puabi, a fey server stopped by with a tray. "Did you want one of the green cocktails?"

Azazel's eyes met the server's.

"With a rosemary sprig in it?"

"You can get that by the gum arabic trees."

Subtle, but something clicked into place for Puabi.

It was a code.

Bowing, the server moved on.

"In a few minutes, I will go join this conversation. It will be all Watcher angels who trust one another. Those left out will be Sam's folk or guests, who could be anyone who obtained an invitation. What you do next depends on you. You are welcome to leave."

She looked up at Azazel through her lashes.

He wore a long tunic of a deep cobalt-blue, with a draped black cloak over it, embroidered with gold. He'd added earrings and more kohl than usual, hair dressed so it shone. He looked edible, and warmth poured upward through her.

My angel.

"Should I? What are my other options?"

"Stand around. Mingle." He darted a glance at the silver-eyed angel.

"Chat them up? Spy?"

"Be careful if you do. Raise a robust shield that is also invisible. They are invasive—they will read your thoughts if they can. Come close, I will give you my protection."

He licked his finger and drew on her forehead the sigil on his necklace. With his wet fingertip on her skin, she wished they were alone. His energy cascaded over her, a breeze that smelled of dark frankincense, below that something earthier.

"You're marking me yours."

"Only for now."

"May I mark you back?"

His eyelashes fluttered.

"Only for now."

Grey-blue eyes searched her face. "Yes."

On his chest, she drew her name in cuneiform with her tongue, flicking one of his nipples. His eyes widened.

"Now go, angel-boy."

After that, she navigated the party. Among the fey folk and angels, she stood out. She was the only incubus-succubus there, animal child of the earth, seductress.

She flirted with anyone pleasant and harmless. She did not pursue Suriyel, but she felt in her skin how they circled the party, closing on her.

After a time, Suriyel appeared at the edge of the group she was in. After a few minutes, her other interlocutors moved away.

Suriyel hovered before her. Closeness emphasized how phosphorescent their silver eyes were. Up close, they appeared less wispy. Like most of the angels, they were strongly muscled, especially their wiry shoulders and arms, shown in an off-white sleeveless robe.

Puabi gave them a hostess smile. "And you are?"

"Moonshadow. You are acquainted with Azazel?"

"A little. I work for him." Joanie had mentioned Alyssa worked with a spirit by that name. Puabi wondered if it was the same one.

A psychic tendril extended, exploring—Suriyel wanted to know more about their acquaintance and didn't want to ask. She enforced her shield subtly, letting the tendril skim off. Suriyel released a breath, their shoulders dropping.

"Yes, I see he has given you his protection. Have you worked for him long?"

"I have not."

"I know him from days long past."

"Mmm?"

The angel reached out a hand tentatively, as if to touch her, then withdrew it. She held her cup of jasmine tea in both hands in front of her, protecting herself.

"We were friends—more than friends. I did things I regret. But I am ready to change."

The gate by the gum arabic trees flew open. The Watcher angels came out as a group, pounding each other's shoulders and ruffling each other's hair, like a team about to play a game.

Suriyel glanced at the group, then back to Puabi.

"So pleasant meeting you. I must go find my friend."

"Of course."

After a few moments, Azazel appeared at her side.

"Anything of note?"

"Your old friend Suriyel did things they regret. But they're ready to change."

"That will happen when the moon falls into the sea."

"What about you? How was the discussion?"

"I may give you details only as you need to know. But it went well."

Chapter 42

A clank, a hiss, heavy breathing sounded. A clash of metal rang out.

Joanie woke a little past midnight.

Another evening, in an infinite near-night sky above her head, djinn fought angels. This happened now every other night or so—sometimes the guard held them off; sometimes it required reinforcements.

Djinni-Max, red and bald-headed, flourished a sword. Thrust, parry, riposte, counterattack flowed back and forth, dancelike.

In the thick of it, Azazel fought in his bronze breastplate and studded leather war-kilt, black wings flared. Beside him, Ekur swung his sword.

With a flying lunge, Azazel engaged one then another djinni, driving them backward. A djinni winked out of the space. The angel who'd fought him turned to another. Bit by bit, the angels drove the djinn out.

Then the fight was done.

She let out the breath she'd held, and yawned. This fighting was all too common; she was losing sleep. Also the djinn kept making power flicker and throwing things off shelves.

Puabi-Ekur and Azazel sheathed their swords and sat down to either side of Joanie.

"This constant fighting is getting old."

"We have a plan," Puabi-Ekur said.

"If we sit here and talk, we'll keep Cleo up. Let me move to my office."

She walked across the dark apartment, trailing her spirits. A ray of light from the parking lot cast her shadow on the kitchen floor. Settling in her office chair, she put her feet on the desk and closed her eyes in meditation.

She found herself in the oasis, on the bench by the palm trees. Full night had fallen, and stars blazed past the aura of lamplight. Puabi-Ekur and Azazel sat to either side of her. Azazel kept his battle dress, though not his wings, but Puabi-Ekur had put on Puabi form and wore a loose black robe.

A wind circled, carrying the scent of woodsmoke and frankincense.

"You need to be free of Max before we go forward. It's never good to fight a war on two fronts. So we talked to Ereshkigal."

Joanie looked from one to the other. A half-smile crossed Puabi's face.

"You both slept with her."

"Well, yeah."

It was rare she could see the incubus-succubus so clearly; mostly Puabi-Ekur was a disembodied voice. Their face shifted subtly, more male, then back.

Angel and succubus shared a glance. A new softness was in Azazel's gaze; the two seemed less wary with each other.

"You also slept with each other."

"Do you mind?" Puabi-Ekur asked.

"No. I just—no." She looked at Azazel. "You were worried Puabi-Ekur didn't trust you. I'm glad you worked that out."

Azazel picked up her hand and kissed it.

"I hope you do not mind, dear one. I showed you the lifetime where we were all together."

"I'm just—it'll take me a moment."

Angling in, Puabi kissed her cheek.

"You are still my Joanie—my Iltani—now and forever." She'd been Iltani in the land of the two rivers, the life they shared so long ago.

Joanie settled into this new knowledge.

She had wanted them to get along. There was always new learning in polyamory. She loved both of them; she loved Cleo and Pete. Each of them had a special, particular place in her heart.

A claw of fear still caught at her.

What if she lost the angel and succubus to each other?

But would that happen? She thought not.

"We talked to Ereshkigal, and that part of the plan's all good. She'll give us the tools to free the angels. I think we need to deal with Max and his djinn friends first."

"Yes, please."

"We shall outline our plan."

Chapter 43

When they finished the outline, Joanie nodded.

"Sounds like it'll work. I'm super sleepy, I should go to sleep."

The angel and the succubus looked at each other over her head.

"My dear one," Azazel said, "I know you wished at one point to spend the night in my arms. Would you grant me an evening to make that wish come true?"

She looked from one to the other.

"And?"

Puabi bit her lip. This was the hard part.

"And wake up with both of us? And see what happens? I know since you and I have been together in this life, your life, we haven't been lovers. Except when I was in Clayton's body, and at that point you thought I was Clayton."

Joanie looked at her under her eyelashes.

"You never asked."

"And if I did ask?"

"You think I would say no to a beautiful spirit who has loved me for millennia, who has always been on my side? Who has protected me and taken care of me? Who I love back? Why would I do that?"

Puabi stared at her, biting her lip.

"First you should sleep."

They walked her to the pavilion along the lane of torches, flames snapping in the breeze. Inside, Azazel glamoured away his battle gear and the fight's dirt, to a loose robe. All three stretched out on the bed's black silk sheets. Reaching out with a current of air, Azazel doused the flames on all but a few candles. Outside the tent, the night wind soughed.

Joanie curled into Azazel's arms, closing her eyes. Azazel enfolded her, deepening into some form of meditation— whatever angels did instead of sleeping.

His movement drew a shine of light along his brown skin, highlighting the pale tracery of scars. They grew heavier as they went up his arms.

He hadn't gotten them all in battle. As part of his imprisonment, as he hung on the wall of the chasm, someone— agents of the Demiurge?—beat him, shredding his wings. The punishment had a sting of humiliation. He was immortal, so he healed, but not without scars.

Now wasn't the time to ask about it.

"I'm going to step outside a moment," Puabi said.

It was full night outside, a clear night. Among the tents of Azazel's followers, fires flickered. Azazel's company always kept watch—this was a shared hell, however unlikely an attack.

Puabi went the other direction, till she found the lip of the chasm. She sat down among the scrub.

Above spun the stars, far clearer than in Joanie's town. It was said Azazel's brother Samyaza hung off Orion, in penance from his life as a fallen angel.

As if in answer, a veil of smoke blew across the stars.

Puabi-Ekur had re-engaged, and here they were—half in love with an angel, always in love with Joanie, soon perhaps to make love to them both.

Things were so good. What was wrong?

Part was facing a long fight. Their plan—to catch Max, deliver him to Ereshkigal, find how to release the fallen angels, and do it—sounded simple, but each step came with opportunities for failure. They'd be scrambling the whole time. It was unlikely Puabi-Ekur or Azazel would be significantly hurt, but they'd have to protect Joanie.

Puabi-Ekur had jumped from a life of utter simplicity, flirting and fucking and moving on, to all this emotion. All this love. For a human, which was frightening enough, but even more frightening for a dark entrapped spirit with more power than theirs.

Their choices were to get used to it, power up somehow and speed through this time, or leave.

Two levels of contract held them, to Azazel and Hekate. To get away from Hekate, they'd have to leave Earth and its sister planets.

They could leave emotionally—tell Azazel they'd keep their contract, but no more sex, no more... burgeoning affection.

They didn't want to be in love. Love was pain. That had been the lesson of all their lives.

A light wind shifted the dust. Everything was dust, dead as the pathways in Ereshkigal's hell.

They'd been a servant only of their own needs for a long time.

This now was, in theory, positive change. But to return to life meant trouble.

In a pause of the wind came the sound of footsteps.

He stopped not far from her, winged form silhouetted against the sky.

"Do you want company?"

She almost said no.

After a moment, she said, "Sure. I could use company."

He sat down beside her, with a questioning look. She gave a slight nod.

He embraced her. She leaned her head on his shoulder.

All this pain. Death had ripped her in two, again and again. Iltani had fallen down a well; Sarah and Maghavatii had burned alive. Was returning worth chancing that kind of loss again? Spirits could be entirely lost, broken by death, or taken too far away to find. Only luck had brought her back to Joanie, and it had been millennia.

Death made humans forget. She remembered.

Face buried in his arm, she cried.

The last time she'd wept, she'd been sitting in Inanna's lap, and each tear had crystallized before falling to dust. This time, she cried liquid tears.

Chapter 44

J oanie woke in the pavilion. The last candlelight stroked the folds of the walls' black silk. Through a gap at the doorway, the light of dawn fell.

Her companions were asleep, so she had a few moments to savor this... well, weird situation, but wasn't that partly why she was a witch and a whore? To get into these situations—louche, debauched, magical. And now on the table was a threesome with a succubus and a fallen angel.

Azazel had magicked away his wings to leave this gorgeous barbarian, tall, too muscled to be slender—dark-olive-skinned, broad shoulders, that beautiful dip at his clavicle, his vulnerable throat. His classical face as beautiful as a woman's was all delicate lines, the bridge of his nose slender. Stubble roughened his cheek. His body lay hidden under covers, one muscled leg thrown out.

How kind he'd been to her. How he'd protected her. All

intertwined with the memory of the deep past, which surfaced in her dreams, when they were husband and wife.

On her other side lay Puabi-Ekur, who'd looked after her for so long—first through and with Clayton, then when she lost Pete. Always Puabi-Ekur was there for her with spirit help and advice.

Puabi's body next to her stretched slender, brown, and lissome, her long, crimped black hair tossed across her smooth back, to her richly curved ass. The dark eyes were closed in sleep, lashes fanned against her smooth cheek, golden earring against her brown neck.

One brown eye opened. Joanie slid over to Puabi, staring at her. Puabi blinked.

A breath, a pause, and she kissed her, the softest touch on soft lips.

Behind Joanie, Azazel moved—was awake, perhaps never had been asleep.

Puabi pushed herself up against the gilt ebony headboard.

"Did you get enough sleep? Are you well-rested? Hungry?"

"Yes, well-rested. Not hungry, or not for food."

She sat up too, nudged Puabi's arm playfully.

Chapter 45

*P*uabi-Ekur faced the other two, sitting cross-legged among the rumpled black-silk sheets.

"Do you want me as a girl or as a boy? Or both?" As neither was possible, too, but didn't seem like something to put on offer, since the object was sex.

"Ooh, I never thought of it like that. We could mix and match."

Puabi-Ekur eyed Azazel. They suspected he could switch it up too, but he didn't volunteer.

Instead, the angel asked, "What do you desire?"

"I'd lean toward being male."

They could become Maelan, the warrior who had been Gus's lover long ago. Of all their incarnations, Maelan was the most even-handed about whom he'd fuck.

But would Maelan appeal to Azazel?

Best stick with what you know.

With a shimmer, they became a masculine version of

Puabi—slender, long-haired, definitely male but young and lissome.

Joanie wiggled over to Puabi the young man, taking his chin, kissed him deeply.

Keeping her arm around Puabi's neck, drawing him with her, she leaned and kissed Azazel.

Puabi slid out of her arm and moved closer to her, kissing her shoulder, stroking her side—staying in the moment, not letting the fear riding them have power.

Joanie traded sides kissing, then brought them both in for a kiss, which turned to licking. Pale dawn light trickled in, added to the golden light of several dozen candles. Licking, touching, nibbling, biting, fingers here, fingers there.

"What do you want?" Puabi whispered.

"Let's just play a bit. I love touching you both."

Taking a handful of his own long hair, Puabi stroked Joanie's back with it as she kissed Azazel. Azazel reached around to take Puabi's arm and pulled him between them. Then both of them were on Puabi, kissing, licking, biting his cheeks, his neck, his sensitive nipples, fingers stroking his arm, his side.

Joanie positioned herself in front of him, stroked his thighs with her fingertips, barely touching. Her fingers moved closer and closer as his cock twitched and grew. At his nod, she licked.

Puabi closed his eyes and dropped back against Azazel, who knelt behind him playing with his nipples, licking and biting his neck, blowing on the sweat there, a tickle of cool.

Behind him Azazel's cock, hard, nudged the crack of his ass.

Joanie's mouth was on him, drawing at him.

"I don't want to come yet." It felt as if it had been centuries.

"What do you want?"

"I don't know. Kiss me."

He tasted his precum on her lips. Azazel enfolded them in his arms.

"I know what I want," Joanie said.

With a gesture of her head, she motioned Azazel behind her.

Looking into his eyes, she kissed Puabi, tongue on tongue, deeper, deeper.

She gently pushed Puabi onto his back and sat astride him, aiming and nudging his cock inside her. She rode him a few beats, then flattened herself along him. Azazel took oil from the side table, slicked it on, maneuvered himself into Joanie's ass. They caught their rhythm and began to move.

Like a climb on a mountain, rising as flame crests and the mountain gives way to fire—everything exploded for Puabi, and a moment later Joanie cried out, and when she spasmed, Azazel shook and groaned.

After a few moments, the angel moved again. Standing up, he grabbed a towel from a pile he'd apparated on the low couch. He crossed back to collapse onto the bed.

The scent of sex floated, sweet as caramel, with undertones of frankincense and sweat.

Puabi found tears in his eyes and wiped them with the back of his hand.

It was love, pure and simple. Scary, but they'd need to learn to live with that.

Chapter 46

With a start, Joanie came to between the incubus and the fallen angel.

Stretching, yawning, she sat up. A whiff of wax drifted from the candles still burning in their gilt candelabra. Some had burned out.

"Now I need food. Then we need to make sure everyone gets their sandwich." She flicked a glance at Azazel. "Don't say you don't want it."

The angel gave her an unreadable look.

"Yeah, right, Mr. I Came Here 'Cause I'm Down to Fuck."

Puabi laughed.

"That's why you're Puabi as a boy, isn't it?"

Puabi demurely hid a smile behind his hand.

He looked across at the angel. "Only if you're comfortable with it, though."

Who knows what had happened to Azazel in all these millennia?

It made her think of Moonshadow—he'd meant to bring

that encounter up, but so much had happened. Now didn't feel like the time.

"Of course," Joanie said. "I don't mean to push. This just makes me happy."

The angel rolled over and stroked her hair, the darkest of chocolate browns, tangled now.

"It has been a long time since I shared myself that way. I had not considered it."

"You can have time to think," Puabi said. "I hope we can reconvene."

"We cannot know. Nevertheless, I do not feel ready for that. I apologize." He turned to Joanie. "What would you like for food, dear one?"

"Ooh—can the pocket hell do eggs sunny-side up with a side of hash browns?"

It took a week of preparation and spellwork to make Max's trap ready. Hannah and Joanie fashioned a wax poppet to represent him. Cleo, Gus, and Hannah helped Joanie magic a heavy length of stainless-steel chain as part of his containment. Azazel and Puabi-Ekur worked on the lead box in the cave in Dudael.

One night, Joanie woke to the clash of arms above her head.

Joanie touched Cleo on the shoulder. With a nod, Cleo got up and tiptoed out of the room. This part was Joanie's show.

Max led the fray, shining bright red, his sword silver in a red mist. Djinn trailed him, shadowy, laughing. The bedroom ceiling hung awash in clouds, past them the other-world sky dark-blue, twenty feet up or more.

The angels followed Azazel's lead. Puabi-Ekur fought as Ekur. Azazel carried a sword she'd seen before, a chunky red stone in its pommel—Max shone scarlet, but Azazel's stone was darker, alizarin crimson.

Metal clashed and rang: thrust, parry, attack, counterattack. Wind circled the room.

One of the angels pierced a djinni, whose shadowy form disappeared. Azazel engaged Max. Max was good, but Azazel was better. He apparated a matching dagger and went after Max with both, only to retreat when Max advanced, playing for time. Another angel took his place.

Joanie watched. Her job right now was to be bait. This was a fight her newborn martial arts skills couldn't touch. And neither djinn nor angels were fully material, just enough to dart out, battle on the mundane plane, then dart back. She held the box and poppet in hand, waiting.

Fallen angels fought off djinn, down to three remaining. Ekur had hung back. Now, as instructed by Azazel, he changed the room, almost imperceptibly. Bit by bit, he made the mundane bedroom into a space fully on the astral plane, pulling the remaining djinn into an astral space. The room smudged and blurred.

If Max's djinn friends noticed, they didn't warn Max.

Another angel pierced another djinni, what would be a killing blow on the material plane. The djinni spun into a cyclone and flew to pieces. Azazel turned with Ekur to Max's last follower.

A series of short attacks rang, blade on blade. The djinni kept off the incubus and angel minute after minute.

Azazel advanced.

Like a dance, like lightning, he thrust, then again, a strike the djinni barely avoided. Azazel chased him from corner to corner of the room, then clove him in two.

The last djinni besides Max disappeared.

With a nod, the angel, incubus, and human witch each jetted from the space.

With a full-body gesture, pushing down, Azazel collapsed astral to earth.

On the Earth plane, Joanie shoved the red-wax poppet into its lead box. She slammed the box shut, closing its prison door.

The planes shifted, with a shake like an earthquake—an implosion. The apartment walls groaned. Something fell with a bang. Smoke seeped from the room's corners with a smell of sulphur. Joanie's ears popped.

Then the dust settled, and the smoke disappeared. The bedroom was just a bedroom again.

It was done.

The box rattled and tumbled as if holding an angry rat. But Max had no escape.

Cleo returned.

"You got him."

From a cardboard container beside the bed, Joanie and Cleo hauled the heavy, dully shining stainless-steel chain. They wrapped it around the box as it bucked and thrashed, each loop of chain helping stabilize it, chanting under their breaths as they did. They locked the ends with a magicked padlock.

Then Joanie put the chain-wrapped box back in the cardboard container, folded it closed, and wrapped a warded besigiled cloth around it. In the kitchen, she put it in a bottom cupboard. It still rattled, but after a while it calmed down.

"That should hold him till we're ready to take him to hell."

Chapter 47

"You're sure this is going to work?"

"Succubus, I am a master magician."

Puabi-Ekur, as Puabi, eyed Azazel. Perhaps he was more worried than he let on, or perhaps she was making him nervous.

Max had been trapped a week as they waited for good astrological weather. Occasionally the box rattled, muffled in its cloth, but it was mostly quiet.

Now, angel and succubus hovered above Joanie, in the all-white kitchen, in the hour and day of Saturn, which Azazel had marked as a good time to take a trapped djinni to hell. A ray of spring sunlight fell through the blue-and-white checkered curtains.

This time of year had more associations with returning from hell than going there, but Max couldn't stay in Joanie's cupboard till fall.

Joanie had warded the house again, both to contain him

and to keep out his friends. So far, it had worked—no djinni had broken their sleep since they'd boxed Max.

"Before all else, I honor earth and sky." Joanie, working naked, raised her knife and cast a witches' circle. Blue flame protected the space.

Cleo stood beside her, robed, helping hold the circle. Kneeling, she opened the cupboard, pulled out the box, set it in the middle of the kitchen floor, and backed away.

Slowly the kitchen filled with dark red light, alizarin crimson, the color of the stone in Azazel's sword pommel, the color of blood.

At a sign from Azazel, Joanie picked up the box.

Azazel stepped forward.

He wore a draped red robe the color of the light. His wings appeared, a black shadow behind him, tightly furled against his body.

Puabi, the fourth in the circle, wore a similar robe in black. Joanie had no idea if Cleo saw Puabi, but Joanie did.

Azazel, a far more powerful spirit, had made himself manifest in the circle, wings folded in the tiny kitchen. He put out his arms, and Joanie set the box into his hands.

They met each other's eyes.

"This piece is done," Azazel said. "We will take him from you."

Puabi put a hand on his elbow.

With a gust of wind, they left the space.

In the kitchen, dust motes circled in a ray of light.

They apparated into the oasis in the middle of the night, in silence and darkness. Breeze stirred among the palm leaves. At Azazel's glance, a few torches lit, casting golden rays across the terracotta tiles.

"You're sure he's still in there."

"Check the box yourself, Puabi-Ekur."

He held out his hands. A dull shine from torchlight fell on its chains. The box rattled and pitched as the captured djinni shook it.

"Then I call you, angel," Puabi said, "to come with me to my Lady Ereshkigal, Queen of the Great Below."

A door to a far building opened, lamps to either side within, black basalt steps down.

How many times had Puabi-Ekur done this? This trip was for Joanie and Gus, and for all whom Max would have tortured given the chance.

Rattling sounded again from the box. Sides dull grey, lead, wrapped with slightly shining chains, it radiated anger.

The gatekeeper opened one gate after another. Word had gone ahead, and no clothing nor jewelry was taken this time.

In sight of the last gate, basalt bound with silver, the box twisted and bucked in Azazel's hands.

Azazel manifested a pair of gauntlets as the box heated to dull red.

They flashed a look at each other and ran down the last steps to Hell's dusty black, cavelike forecourt. Ereshkigal sat on her throne, black chalcedony glinting. Seeing the situation at a glance, she let out a piercing whistle.

A crew of galla ran forward. Two held a net, woven of some black substance, which they threw over the box as Azazel let it fly.

The box fell with a clank to the stone floor, suddenly alive, thrashing and bucking. The black net tightened around it. The galla secured it and hauled it off along a long, curving path.

Puabi-Ekur and Azazel prostrated themselves before Ereshkigal.

"You may rise, my dears. Thank you for the present! The galla always like new challenges, and we have not had such a one for centuries."

Far away, the box flailed in its adamantine net.

"Don't worry, dear angel. It is our business to trap men's souls. He will be judged, almost certainly punished. The galla enjoy that."

"My lady, Queen of the Great Below, a million thanks to you for keeping this being that has tormented our friends."

"I trust you will show your thanks," Ereshkigal purred. Curled into her basalt throne, she'd manifested as a Sumerian queen in a draped linen gown, huge dark eyes ringed with kohl.

"Of course, my lady. You mentioned also tools of special sanction. We would love to obtain such a thing, though as you say the human witch must wield it."

The goddess tapped red-rouged lips with a bony finger.

"Not so fast, beautiful angel. The witch must be worthy of the weapon."

"And how shall we determine that, my lady?"

"I need to meet her. Question her."

Did Joanie need to die?

Ereshkigal rolled her eyes.

"In ritual space will do. But first... you mentioned thanks."

Chapter 48

The evening after they took the box, Joanie meditated in her office before bed.

Cleo had gone to sleep early—she'd probably need to go into work at least part of Sunday. Joanie had Sunday off.

Lamplight low, she centered her attention on her coral-colored Inanna candle.

She deepened into meditation. Puabi-Ekur appeared, a dark wisp without solid form.

"Come with me to the pocket hell. The three of us need to talk."

She let Puabi-Ekur lift her up, and out, while her body went deeper into trance.

At the oasis, they met black darkness, a few stars. A strand of cloud crossed, the scent of woodsmoke. Puabi-Ekur, as Puabi, led her along the lane of torches. At the end, its silhouette cut against night, stood the two-story silk pavilion. With a whisper of cloth opening, they entered, to the flicker of candles.

Kissing Joanie, the angel sat next to her on the couch, gave her wine and dates. Puabi threw herself on the bed. They told the story of their descent with Max.

"We did not see Max judged, but that will come. He will not leave Ereshkigal's realm soon."

Puabi hung off the bed upside-down, bent backward at the waist.

"But for the next step," she said, "Ereshkigal wants to talk to you, to test you."

"That's reasonable, I guess."

"She'll want something in exchange. I think at the very least you'd need to agree to be her priestess."

"I don't mind that. I work with her sister already, and I've worked with Hekate, who's syncretized with her."

Puabi rolled over to look her in the eye. "I'm not sure how active a priestesshood she wants."

Angel and succubus exchanged a look.

"What are you not telling me?"

"There are various offers you might put on the table."

"I see." They had both had sex with Ereshkigal, clearly in payment. "I am a whore."

The angel pulled a hand through his long hair. "She is sexually hungry."

"She's also not above quizzing you about where you are with your spiritual work. She does talk to her sister. I thought I'd do you the favor of quizzing you first."

Joanie groaned.

"I'm nowhere with it. You know that."

Puabi propped chin on palm, elbow balanced on her knee.

"I'm giving you a chance to get your story straight before we go to the Great Below."

"I meditate sometimes. I work with my coven."

"What would you say is your spiritual calling? You apparently have an incubus-succubus as a spirit guide—why would that be?"

"Stop it. I get it."

She'd dragged her feet for ages—what made her? Fear. Whoring was beyond the pale, whoring for the goddess even more so.

Fear was a poor excuse but a real one.

Azazel flicked a glance at Puabi.

"Azazel, they're right. They've been suggesting for a while I get on with it. Sacred whoredom."

"If I were going to go meet the Queen of Hell, I would set up a small shrine to her and consider how I was going to reinvigorate my spiritual practice. There is the poison path too, and your work with Nora—you volunteered to help with the witch farm."

Azazel smirked. "Perhaps I can arrange an introduction to my brother Samyaza, the angel of root-cutting."

"He teaches magic, too," Puabi said, leaning forward. "Azazel, that is. That could be part of it."

"And invented makeup. I know. Maybe I can get makeup tips." Joanie frowned. "What's up, y'all? I said I would help."

"We just want you to be ready for Ereshkigal. She can be intimidating."

She locked eyes a moment with Puabi, then turned to Azazel.

"Are you worried?" she asked.

"Yes."

"What about?"

"I hope with your support, and that of Inanna and Ereshkigal, I can accomplish something I have long desired for my people. I will be fearful of the outcome until it is accomplished."

She stroked his arm, warm, sliding her finger along an ancient scar.

"Anything I can do for you and for the angels who protected me, I will do. Not for reciprocity. For love."

The angel almost smiled.

"Hey, also, I meant to say—one of my coven has a spirit guide, an angel, Moonshadow, who came to me in a class meditation. Someone who knew you from before. They weren't good at boundaries."

Azazel frowned. "Describe them."

"Very tall, very pale, silver eyes."

"I know who that is. You shielded against them, yes?"

"Yes."

"Do not worry. I have protections in place."

"But who are they?"

"A spy for the Demiurge."

The coral-colored candle still flickered in her office. It was her Inanna candle, though often she only said a cursory hello to her goddess.

Now she had homework: a little altar to the Goddess of Hell, and a plan for her magical future.

What to do was obvious. Start the Inanna shrines again. She'd been talking about that forever.

Follow the poison path.

Follow the dream that someday she'd have her witch farm.

Ditch capitalism faster than she was, however insidious and alluring it was. Though she'd have to keep the day job for now—perhaps for a while—and having started the accounting degree, it would be stupid to stop. Money wasn't going away anytime soon.

In her next meditation, a couple days later, Puabi-Ekur passed her the latest word from Ereshkigal.

"She wants to see you alone."

"I can do that."

She'd do a lot for someone she cared for. So many people had been there for her. Pete had died for her.

The angels deserved their freedom.

"You know the traditional approach, right?"

"I read the liturgy." Inanna had descended through the gates, undressing herself of the tokens of queenship as she went to her sister.

"You probably want someone to talk you into trance, and keep watch after you. Someone who can call you back if something goes wrong."

Cleo would do that for her.

"Do you think something will go wrong?"

"You are going to Hell. It's something to take seriously."

"I do."

Though she was used to talking to intimidating people while naked, she dressed up before she went to see the Queen of the Great Below. It seemed only right.

As a base, she put on a dark-purple slip dress, such as she might wear to meet a new client. For makeup, she didn't go heavy, but chose a dark shaping cat-eye line and purple lipstick the color of the dress. As when planning a game of strip poker, she made sure to dress in layers—long black gloves, a bolero shrug, plenty of jewelry.

In her office, she added a small altar on a bookshelf, draped in black, with its own incense burner. To it, she fed Mesopotamian incense: cedar, juniper, cypress, tamarisk. She drew and framed an image of the goddess, at her feet coiled a set of blue beads the color of lapis lazuli.

Cleo had agreed to be her meditation guide and keeper. She wanted to be there to protect her girl.

They'd pulled out the futon, which took up most of the room, and Joanie reclined on it. Cleo sat on the desk chair.

"Make yourself comfortable. Take some deep breaths. You're getting more and more relaxed...."

Chapter 49

The scent of dust rose to her nostrils. The black basalt steps went down and down and down—a hint of red to them, like the chasm where Azazel hung.

She left her clothes with the gatekeeper, a layer at each gate. At the stairway's foot, she stood naked and barefoot in a wide, dark, dusty expanse, the only light a faint glow of red.

A huge throne sat in front of her, basalt inlaid with black chalcedony, empty.

She knelt before it, folded prostrate, arms stretched before her, waiting.

She knelt there a long time. She thought of Azazel hanging on the wall of Dudael. She counted breaths, falling deeper into trance.

Around her collected a set of galla: grey, pointed-eared, naked, heads topped with horns, carrying long, sharp-pointed tridents.

"What's thisssssss?!" The shriek went painfully high.

A sibilant growl: "It'sssssss a living human girl!"

"We don't get thosssssssssse much!"

They circled her, poking her with the tridents, prick of needles when these pierced her flesh—just that for now. She jumped a little at each poke.

She needed to keep it together until the Lady appeared. Ereshkigal had asked for her visit.

"Interesting! I wonder why she's down here!"

The needle-sharp points drew blood.

"She doesn't have an ally, or much protection."

"But she's not dead!"

They poked and poked, like biting flies.

A jab went deeper.

"Ow!"

"We could fuck her. Sometimes they like that. Or at least they scream."

One grabbed her arm, flipped her onto her back, and leapt on top of her. It smelled like rotting garbage, and she retched. A huge spiked thing poked at her pussy.

Then the air changed, and there was someone on the throne.

A deep voice said, "Leave us, galla." It echoed in the cave-like space. They scattered.

"Stand, human woman."

Joanie stood up, tamping down her fear. A skeletal, black-robed form sat on the throne, head a skull with deep-set red eyes, horizontal black pupils like some kind of mad goat's.

A shudder went through her.

"You have come here on sufferance, but know that I could take your soul."

"Your majesty, I am deeply in your debt for this audience."

"So you are."

She cast her eyes down—a direct look might be taken as a challenge.

How could she get from here to her proposition? She couldn't let the mission fail because of her.

"My lady Ereshkigal, I would offer you anything for the tools to free Lord Azazel's people."

"Anything! You've been coached for this task."

Stung, she looked up.

"Not in that part. I truly desire this, my lady."

The red eyes stared at her.

"My lady, for this I would offer you a lifetime of service. I have made you an altar. I would do more."

The lady lounged in her chair. "The altar was acceptable. How much more would you do?"

"Let me show you."

She advanced to the throne and knelt before it.

"May I?"

Ereshkigal hiked her robe up skeletal thighs, exposing a red vulva.

"You can try."

She stroked the bony thighs, gently licked.

She warmed to her task. She was a professional.

She licked and bit gently, nudged the tips of her fingers inside her, but the goddess shook her head and she retracted them. She sped up, as quickly as she could, saliva mixing with the goddess's liquids.

When Ereshkigal came, the entire Great Below shook.

A pause. She watched the goddess's face. Her great eyes were shut.

Joanie dropped back to kneeling, folding her hands in her lap.

The goddess switched to the aspect of a Sumerian queen, huge dark eyes now open.

"Very well. I'll give you what you desire." She gestured, and Joanie rose. "There's no need to test you at this point—your trials are ahead of you."

Shit. Something she didn't want to know. "What do you mean?"

"Do you need more trials?"

"No, my lady."

Ereshkigal put a finger under her chin, tipped her head back; after a long stare, she kissed her, filling her mouth with tongue. Joanie shivered.

"I shall not give you to the galla. I like you, little human." She stood from the throne. "Follow me."

They climbed through Hell along a dusty path. Joanie kept her head down, glad to be moving forward. A pale red light followed the goddess, illuminating the way, strewn with black basalt boulders. No denizens—perhaps they knew to get out of the way. A walled garden glowed with muted jewel tones, but they passed it.

They approached a small building, its black marble veined with red. Silver bound the door and limned the tops of the pillars that fronted it. A heavy chain and padlock secured the door, but with a wave from the queen these fell open.

Inside, it was black-dark. At the goddess's gesture, two silver lamps burst into flame. Ereshkigal went up low steps to a plinth, where lay a long, grey-black basalt box inlaid with diamond-pattern mosaics. At another gesture, the stone top slid off, settled to lean at the far side.

"Come here," the goddess said. Joanie moved to Ereshkigal's side.

The stone space was filled with boxes and items wrapped in black linen. From these, Ereshkigal took a dark-stained wooden casket. This too was beautifully inlaid, with contrasting pale wood and silver, lions and bulls standing upright.

She opened it, setting the top on the edge of the plinth. In the box, on a linen pad, gleaming in lamplight, lay a knapped obsidian knife.

"I give you one of my treasures. There are only a few of these in the world."

Joanie looked up into her face.

"I will do my best, Lady."

"You don't know your own strength, little human. I believe you equal to wielding it."

Something rustled in the black stone box on the plinth, as if something in it was alive.

"It has the particular quality of being able to open a door for spirits, to whatever their next plane is—punishment, challenge, return to Earth. To use it, simply cut a door into the air. Be sure to state it's only for those authorized, although the knife also does that itself. Draw the knife back over the cuts to close the door."

The rustling grew louder. The Lady glared into the sepulcher, and it stopped.

"Obviously, you can't carry the box around all the time. I will give you the ability to access it. Hold out your arm."

She did, palm up.

The Lady drew a bony, black-nailed finger along it.

At a lightning slash of pain, Joanie cried out.

The knife lay incised, tattooed on her inner arm: a simple blackwork design, powerful and blunt.

She looked up, wide-eyed, and the Lady kissed her, reaching to stroke her vulva. Joanie leaned into the fingers, releasing herself to lust.

"You want me, don't you, little human? You didn't expect that. Truly you are one of mine. However."

The goddess stepped back, freeing her. She almost fell over.

"You have work to do in the upper world. When you need the knife, touch your mark and call for it. I'll return you now—no need for the long climb."

The goddess licked her fingers, then kissed her again—Joanie tasted herself.

"Until we meet again."

In a moment, she opened her eyes.

She sat up, shaking her head to clear it, and turned her arm.

Her flesh was still marked with Ereshkigal's knife.

hrough two weeks of work and accounting classes, through meditations and prayers to Inanna and Ereshkigal, through the hours of Nora's class, she stayed preoccupied. She wanted to free Azazel's legions now.

"Patience, Saadiya."

Azazel wanted the right astrological timing for this project, which he'd worked on for hundreds of years.

"I desire a waxing moon, and nothing in too harmful an aspect. Jupiter and Venus need to be moderately happy. The idea is to free my people, and I want the greater and lesser benefics' help."

Joanie had introduced him to Cleo in guided meditation —they'd nodded to each other warily. Cleo, Hannah, Nora, Gus, and Alyssa had agreed to be present for the ritual where they released the angels, to help hold and defend the space. Now Azazel had visited her in a dream.

In his arms, she felt protected, and she wished she could

give him that. At least she'd gotten the knife.

Puabi-Ekur lay on her other side, sated, drowsing.

"How may I make you happy in the meantime?" Azazel asked.

Joanie glanced over at the incubus-succubus, once again in boy-Puabi mode.

"I would love to watch Puabi-Ekur fuck you. Or perhaps even do it myself."

The angel gave her a long look.

"Shall I tell you the story of why I do not want to do that?"

Images shot into her mind—Azazel held down by angels all silver and gold and white. Blood ran down his muscular legs.

"Let us say Yaldabaoth's minions are not as sweet as sometimes thought."

"Oh, beloved." She stroked his cheek. "I never want you to be unhappy."

The grey-blue eyes looked past her.

"Too late, star of heaven."

In the spring night, clear, cold for April, frost predicted, Orion had set. A sprinkling of stars sparkled across the zenith. The west lay faintly lit, almost green.

At Hannah's house, too early for roses, the daffodils hung on, later varieties in bloom, white and orange. Flowering plums scattered pink shreds across the street.

Coming from work early, Joanie met Hannah at the door.

"I'm just doin' some dishes."

"I can help dry."

Hanging up her coat, she walked into the kitchen, rolling up her sleeves.

There, on her forearm, lay the tattoo of the knife, a strong visual mark of the uncanny. It wasn't going anywhere.

Beside her, Hannah bent over the sink.

"I went down to see Ereshkigal, like I told you I was going to? I wanted to show you something."

She stretched out her arm.

"When did you get that?"

"She put it on me!"

They met each other's eyes.

"A mentor of mine said, if you're doin' it right, the life of a witch should be fantastic, beyond the reach of normal humans."

"If that's the yardstick, I'm winning."

Having dried a rackful of dishes, Joanie went to build the fire in the backyard.

She felt shy about this ritual. This angel was her boyfriend; everyone was coming at her request. She hated to be the one asking. Yet hadn't she done her bit for each of them?

She didn't like to be the center of attention; it meant trouble.

She layered down paper, tinder, kindling—bits from an old wooden crate—and half a wax-and-sawdust log.

A fire in this basket was how it had begun, and Azazel greeting her in the darkness.

She added two small logs of sweet-smelling fir, gummy at points with resin.

Giving in to temptation, knowing Hannah had a full

woodpile, she lit the fire. Flames twisted upward. She put chilly fingers above them.

She reached out on the astral, and the angel rushed to her, wrapping his arms around her in the darkness. Lips brushed her cheek. On the other side was a dark shape, Puabi-Ekur. They consistently appeared together now, which made her smile. She wanted them to be happy.

Cleo appeared, came in for a hug. "Your people are here," she whispered.

"They are."

Cleo glanced a moment into darkness. "I guess we'll all need to get comfortable with each other."

"It can be don't ask, don't tell."

"That's never been my style."

People were gathering. Alyssa poked her head out the back door. A lunar wisp floated behind her a moment, then disappeared.

Joanie collected the things for the altar. This most important of rituals was happening at last.

Hannah cut the first circle, Joanie the next, Hannah the third.

Hannah called in the Star Goddess first, as she had at the first Watchers ritual. Now Orion was in hiding, gone right after sunset.

Joanie called in Ereshkigal, "Lady of the Great Below, gifter of the knife, come to us if you will for honor and worship." For her, she lit Mesopotamian incense.

Then she called in the Watchers, starting with her angel.

"Hail, Azazel, most beloved, bringer of gifts. Accept my heartfelt offerings for yourself and your brothers and sisters."

As they had before, she gave the fire frankincense, wine, and raw meat. The frankincense burned up, so fast she barely smelled it. The wine sent the fire into a blue flare. The meat sizzled.

The circle watched the meat fry. Beyond the witches, the Watcher company collected. Silhouettes faded in and out of darkness—Azazel's angels who'd come to Earth with him so long ago. Hints of gold reflection shone, mail or a breastplate or sword pommel gilt by firelight.

Behind her stood Azazel, invisible but with arms wrapped around her. Puabi-Ekur was a curl of smoke in the aether next to her.

She tapped her arm and invoked the knife into her right hand, black-hilted, blue-black light shining on its silver-honed edge.

"I open this door to provide these spirits freedom, to let them move on to their appointed next realm. The door is only for those the Star Goddess and Ereshkigal deem ready for this change."

She raised the knife, and in the aether made a cut, an edge of fire with a shining light beyond. A cut each for the top, side, bottom, and the door opened.

The company moved toward it. One angel slipped through to their destination.

Bam!

A blast of sound ricocheted, a concussion in the air, a white explosion.

Angels, bundles of dark wings, flew backward. On Azazel's face was an open-mouthed shout—she lost it in the noise.

Utter light broke to complete darkness.

Chapter 51

*J*oanie came to, blank-headed and cold.

It was the middle of the night. Clouds barred the black sky. Invisible bonds held her, midair, against an invisible pillar—in astral form only, her body far away, asleep or passed out. The silver cord to return was missing.

Far across the bowl of the sky, Azazel led his legions, a delta of black against a formation of feathered white. So far away, she heard nothing. Occasionally an explosion flashed, but mostly they fought by spear and sword.

These white-feathered angels had to be servants of the Demiurge, fighting to keep Azazel's legions trapped.

Five white-winged angels faced every black-winged one. Azazel's folk each took on two or three and won. When each angel fallen or unfallen took a mortal blow, they disappeared as the djinn had, she guessed to another plane.

Tumult roiled across the sky; angels plummeted and were erased.

She found Azazel by his wingspan, the number of white angels fighting him, and the encircling winds whipping at his foes.

Wheeling, ducking, diving, rising, the battle flowed across the sky from one horizon to the other.

High above the palms, in the air of the pocket hell, angels fought like birds at war. Puabi-Ekur, as Ekur, stayed near Azazel.

Disembodied to the point of contact, then a black blur, he fought with a short sword and knife, invisible, a wisp—his essential self. He chopped down these feathered fools each time they tried to kill his angel.

Ekur fought at Azazel's back, diving and leaping and backing to avoid the huge black wings. He shoved one angel off and stabbed him in the gut, to a cut-off cry. The angel fell away. He slashed another, a long cut along a feathered wing. That one pinwheeled down to the desert brush, then disappeared. Each time, at the mortal blow, the enemy winked out, snuffed like a candle flame.

Feathers drifted down with the scent of blood, the stench of sweat. He whirled to chop the arm off a white-feathered one who'd lunged at Azazel. Push, slash, cut, stab, again and again. Occasionally, some white-winged soldier managed to touch them, but they skittered away.

Momentary triumphs punctuated fear and rage. A flash of glance from his lover made connection. They fought well together. A cut stung his forehead, a worse slash on his leg, but in the constant fight he had no time to pay attention.

Wave after wave of white angels came at them. Both sides were immortal. But having wed themselves to earth, fallen angels tired more quickly, once away took more time to recover—too long to return to this battle.

A shove, a slash, a reach, a lunge, a stab.

White-winged forces cut through Azazel's folk. Joanie watched, biting her lip, periodically struggling against the bindings, which wouldn't give.

A new flight of dark wings—another Watcher angel and their legion—entered from the far horizon. They'd found a summoner to call them. Her heart leapt.

But just as they did, Azazel plummeted from the sky, a death-dive, black flames flying.

Oh, my beloved.

A blow hit her head, and she saw no more.

Half-awake in darkness, still on the astral, she was being carried by some monstrous white bird.

No, an angel.

The other kind of angel.

To the flapping of wings, cold air washed her face. Sky-landscape flew by, black on grey on black—grey clouds, black sky.

Her captor looked down and saw she was awake. A gesture, a sparkle passed before her eyes, and she was out again.

When she opened her eyes, she was in a gilded cage, alone.

Around her, peach-pink tinted clouds, puffed and full, slowly skated across a fair blue sky. Dawn rather than sunset, if she had to guess.

She lay on a pallet covered in white linen, still in spirit form, wearing an ankle-length white robe. She was clean, felt no hunger or pain.

She felt nothing.

She looked up. The cage was suspended by a length of golden chain that disappeared into the ice-cream-castle clouds, no less a prison for being pretty.

Standing, she went to the edge, tried putting her hand through the gilded bars. She might be able to squeeze through, throw herself out—to what end, she had no idea, but she didn't want to stay here.

But though she could push into the space past the bars, it resisted her, as if it was made out of stiff gelatin or plastic. She could only get a few inches past the bars.

She sat back on the pallet.

She tried reaching out on the astral, but met the equivalent of the wall of gelatin—utterly shut down. She made no contact with Azazel or Puabi-Ekur or anything else, only got white noise.

She lay back on the pallet and stared into the clouds.

After a time, she went back to sleep.

She had no idea how much time passed like that. But it was a long time.

When she woke, she never felt hungry, or thirsty, never needed to pee.

She sat waiting, hanging in nothingness.

The clouds moved, flickered, but the light never changed, and she never saw direct sun. Neither did she see birds, or angels.

She passed the time in memories, half-dreams, sometimes singing. Anger welled up, but she let it go. It did no good.

She did her best to sleep. When she slept, she had no dreams.

Chapter 52

Someone stood within the open door of her cage. She sat up.

Perhaps seven feet tall, golden-haired, their white-feathered wings gently moving behind them, her visitor was unearthly in their beauty.

"Be not afraid."

She glowered. "Don't worry. I'm fine."

"You are required at audience."

She stood. Steely blue eyes gauged her. She met them, gritting her teeth.

Fuck these guys. They had no right.

The angel picked her up in their arms as if she weighed nothing, took off with her across the pastel sky, their wings flapping like the snapping of a flag in the breeze.

After a time, she saw a white tower ahead, held up on a single, impossibly tall white pillar that curved to a flat top, the whole looking like modernist furniture.

They flew up to it, and the angel set her down on the lip

of a wide-open foyer. The angel gestured her to follow, and she trailed the white feathery wings along walkways of pure white stone with the slight graininess of unpolished marble, wide enough she didn't fear falling into the oblivion of blue sky to either side.

After a long walk, they came to a wider platform of white stone. On three sides, all was sky. Diffuse white light flooded the space, with a bright solid light burning ahead, like a star, at the edge of the platform, too bright to look at.

To one side, wrapped in a pile of golden chains, stood Azazel, wingless. Beside him stood Puabi-Ekur as Puabi, cuffed around wrists and feet with a line of golden links between. Both wore white robes.

They must have struggled more, to be chained. Or they were feared more.

The white-winged angel walked her forward, and she searched her lovers' faces. Azazel was far away, in some hell of his own, but he acknowledged her with a flick of lashes. Puabi's dark eyes burned fire—she was as pissed as Joanie.

This was wrong.

She broke and ran for her people. But in one flying swoop, the angel caught her midsection. She struggled against the adamantine grip but couldn't get free. The angel dragged her toward the front of the space.

They approached a huge throne, grey-veined white marble, dressed and decorated in gold, rays flared behind it. The back of the throne went up two stories. The light came from the throne seat, as if a star sat in it, too bright to look at.

Ordinary people were not allowed to see Yaldabaoth—the Demiurge. She was here, so what did that mean? Was she dead?

I don't care. This is bullshit.

The angel hauled her closer—still a long way to go. To either side of the throne stood a host of feathered beings, some solid and clear, some glimmering, half-there. She glimpsed Moonshadow, but they disappeared among the throng.

She couldn't face the light straight-on, so she glanced at it sideways, out of the corner of her eye. There, in flickers, she saw what the light hid.

Like a child in a huge seat, on the throne sat a small-built man, slouched like a crumpled bit of laundry at its base. He had a goofy half-grin on his face, and his white hair went every direction. He wore a white linen suit, loose and wrinkled, a pale-pink carnation in his buttonhole. He looked like a chancer, someone who'd rolled high somehow and was playing out the game.

He wasn't at all what she'd expected.

The angel stopped, let go their grip on her. Her midsection was sore—it would be bruised.

Another pair of angels chivvied Azazel and Puabi over to stand beside Joanie.

She hated this manhandling, this place, but to be in the aura of her people calmed her.

Out of the great white light boomed a voice.

"You have defied me, and now you see the consequences of your actions."

Azazel shook his long hair back. His wings, black shadows, now flickered behind him.

"You have once again foiled the attempt of my followers to continue on their spiritual path," he replied.

"And ever shall. You are fated to lose this battle, Azazel."

The fallen angel stood straighter.

His golden chains snapped, kept for show till he chose to break them. Now his wings flared, shockingly black against white marble and blue sky.

"I do not believe so. Millennia ago, my sibling Watchers and I fought amongst ourselves. Now we are united. Do you want this war? You surprised us once, but that will not happen again."

Wings rustled as the white-feathered angels glanced at each other.

"We have the power to combat you. You never wiped out all our children. We are great upon the earth, great enough to challenge you and win. Do you want that?"

Joanie stepped forward.

"Why still punish the legions of angels who only followed their leaders for love? They've done penance for millennia. Are you really just a bully?"

The light blazed up and out, as if trying to scare her. She held her ground.

Azazel eyed her. His lip twitched—he almost smiled.

"I knew you long ago," Azazel said to Yaldabaoth, "and I do not believe you are only a bully. Long ago, we were of the same company. You know my people's worth. Make a gesture of good faith. Let them go."

Puabi flared like a dark fire.

"I too know you of old, Yaldabaoth. Release Azazel's people. At least get out of their way."

The star blazed on the throne, silent.

The white-winged angels shifted on their feet, watching each other.

I won't be captured again.

Joanie tapped the inside of her forearm, and the blue-black knife slid into her hand.

With a swing of her arm, she cut top, side, and bottom. The door opened to golden fire. Azazel broke Puabi's chains with a swipe of his hand, and the three of them leapt into the light. Twisting, Joanie drew the knife along the three cuts to close the door.

The flames died, to utter darkness. She held tight to Puabi's and Azazel's wrists.

They fell and fell, in the wind of their falling, through utter darkness, on and on and on.

Maybe they would fall forever.

Out of nowhere so she couldn't brace for it, impact knocked the wind out of her. Brown dust exploded. She lay in dirt.

After a moment, gasping, she sat up.

She lay in the dust of the path that threaded the pocket hell, in front of her the low brown buildings, behind her the stand of palms with their bench.

Her two beloveds lay beside her. As she watched, Puabi sat up, shaking the dust out of her hair. Azazel pushed himself to his haunches. His black wings flared out, shook to right themselves, folded, and disappeared.

Standing, she looked around.

It was the middle of the night. A breeze shook the palm leaves.

Chapter 53

*W*ings exploded above them, white, silver-threaded, a fog like moonlight.

Fuck.

They'd been followed.

Azazel shouted a war-cry, calling his angels. Puabi-Ekur shifted instantly to Ekur and fighter mode. He turned to Joanie.

"You have to go."

"How do I get out?"

"Go in one of the side buildings. Meditate yourself out."

They stared at each other a split second.

"I love you."

"I love you."

Joanie ran toward the cluster of mudbrick structures.

Ekur turned to fight beside Azazel, who was again hovering, a phantom. The oncoming formation was led by the angel of the moon: Moonshadow—Suriyel. Tall as a mountain, shining pale light, milky-white, they wielded a blade curved like the sickle moon.

They struck at Azazel.

"Call in reinforcements!" Ekur shouted. The Watchers would help.

"They are bound to their hells unless called!"

"I can reach Samyaza."

"I need you here!"

Ekur jumped in.

Suriyel fought leaping and spinning—a fog enveloped them, hiding their movements, slowing their enemies. Their sickle blade sliced through the fog to strike. A company like them emerged from their mist, bladed with sickle swords. Some threw night lighting, some metal stars.

Azazel's element, the wind, broke the fog and blew it away. He fought with the longsword. Much of his company brought the same, some other weapons: one a long whip like a scirocco wind, one the power of the cyclone. At what would have been a mortal blow, the white-winged angels winked out, to nothing.

The wind chased away the fog, and the battle appeared, laid out before them. Azazel had forty legions. Twice or three times that followed Suriyel—half the host of heaven.

Suriyel's voice came as a pervading whisper, through the air, through the ground beneath them.

"You are my beloved. I have never forgotten you. I have never not loved you. Come away from the rotting earth. Come back to the love of God. Come back to me."

Against the whispering, Azazel shouted:

"The Earth is my home! Here I will stay. The true creator loves the created."

Grunts, shouts, cries of pain bounced by them, source obscured by mist. Wind cut into fog. Ekur and Azazel battled as a pair, once again back to back. Ekur fought with short sword and knife. Azazel brandished his longsword, with a buckler he used also to punch. With a blow, a white-winged angel fell away. Ekur stabbed another, who dropped, blinking to nothingness. A hot coppery scent of blood hung in the air. His shoulder throbbed, a slash into the muscle. Another came out of the fog, at Azazel. With a flash of fear, he cut that one away. He guarded Azazel with everything he had.

Slowly the fog, the sickles, the burning stars pushed Azazel's warriors back. Though they were in their appointed hell, they could be too badly injured to fight. They took longer to recover than the white-winged folk; if the battle took long enough, the others could return. Neither side could fully win, but they could wear each other down, till leaders called a stop.

"I must go," Ekur said, low in Azazel's ear. "We need help."

Two more angels attacked Azazel. He flung himself sideways, but a sickle slashed his side. He roared.

"Go quickly!"

To the garden overflowing with irises and crocuses, flame trees rustling by the wall, they went as Puabi, so Samyaza would remember.

She touched down on gravel. Half the space away, on a couch, Samyaza lay surrounded by attendants, in deshabille, winecup tipped over beside him. Seeing Puabi approached, he threw on a robe and stood.

"Leave us," he told his hangers-on.

Even with wings hidden, he towered over her, green and purple snaking in his long black hair.

"I recognize you. You came to the party with Azazel."

"I did. You know Lord Azazel wants to release his legions. Our companion Joanie was gifted by Ereshkigal with a knife to open their path. But the Demiurge's angels stopped that and captured us three. Joanie freed us, but angels pursued us. My lord begs you to help us fight."

"Yes, of course. Consider my company summoned, little succubus." A glance grazed her bust and hips. "I will call our friends. We can approach their numbers. And we are better fighters."

In a heartbeat, Puabi-Ekur returned to Azazel as Ekur, took up their place again at his back—cutting off a killing blow with his sword. Azazel's flank dripped blood.

Metal rang on metal. Ekur thrust, and a white angel dropped.

Samyaza's legions poured into the fray. The pocket hell teemed with angels—at the oasis, in the fields beyond the tents, in the air above. Beings winged with black, bronze, green, and purple clashed with those white-winged.

Samyaza's legions fought with mace, whip, bow, and sword. A legion wielded tangling vines; archers rained biting snakes.

In the infighting, back to back with Azazel, it was grunt, stab, shove. One white angel fell, then another, disappearing into dark. Angel blood flowed bright as humans'. Ekur thrust into a white midsection with a grunt; that one was gone. A slash, a chop—two gone. Azazel bashed another on the head with his buckler. Another dropped away.

A brief pause fell. Ekur let Azazel's wind dry sweat off his forehead.

Azazel gestured to a new group of angels that burst into the sky, midnight blue among falling stars.

"Kokabiel's people, stellar angels." Explosions, works of fire, took whole rows of white wings out.

Suriyel's main troop flew to meet Kokabiel's. Azazel and Ekur soared upward through the battle, fighting vertically—slashing, cutting, stabbing. A cry—an angel fell, wing broken. A lunge, and another tumbled.

From the height of the storm, Puabi-Ekur looked down.

White angels still far outnumbered dark.

Chapter 54

Standing beside Cleo in the doorway, Hannah looked down at Joanie. Gus and Alyssa stood behind her.

In the white bedroom, silver-spangled, the bed all tousled sheets, a sour smell of sickness hung.

At the Watchers ritual, when Joanie cut the door she'd fallen down in deep trance. Hannah had recommended treating her like someone on a witch-journey, dosed with flying ointment, who might be out a day or more. At the end of the evening, they bundled her into her car and Cleo drove her home.

But the trance hadn't broken. It had been two days now.

"On and off, she's had a fever," Cleo said. "I started thinking maybe she got the flu or some other virus."

"She should go to the ER."

Unspoken was that taking Joanie to a hospital, with her uninsured, would mean debt they'd be paying off for months, maybe years. She hadn't spent the extra money on student insurance—every few dollars made a difference on her salary. But she'd stalled on joining the state health care plan, since the website was so often down. She'd counted on youth and luck, but her luck had run out.

"She looks awful," Gus put in.

Hannah's and Cleo's eyes met.

"She belongs in a hospital."

Cleo sighed. "You're right."

"We'll help carry her to the car."

Chapter 55

In the small oasis building, lamp glow falling, on a bench inset in the wall, Joanie tried to meditate. Screams and cries outside made it hard to focus.

After a while, she stopped trying. She drifted to the door to watch the battle. Such huge armies—the swath of it made her gasp. Part of her wanted to go fight. But she had no weapons and little skill.

Bit by bit, the white angels cut through the dark. One Watcher follower could take half a dozen Demiurge angels. But the fallen angels were fewer, and earth-nature slowed them.

She couldn't let her people be defeated. She had Ereshkigal's knife, which cut you through to the plane you needed to go to. Maybe from here she didn't need it; she could simply go to Ereshkigal. The goddess would be happy to see her.

"Ereshkigal!"

A small space opened. The Lady reached out a hand and pulled her through.

In the dusty, black forecourt of Hell, Ereshkigal lounged on her throne, with its dull sheen of basalt, inset black chalcedony gleaming. She appeared as a queen of Sumer, the linen of her dress sheer to see-through. Around the throne, the dead wandered in crowds, listless and staring. She'd set Joanie on the step before her.

"I hear the sound of battle behind you."

"That's Azazel and Puabi-Ekur and Watcher angels fighting angels from the Demiurge. Though it's a little complicated." Something dawned on her. "Hey, can I ask you for help?"

"In this conflict?"

"Is that possible?"

"Technically, Azazel's realm is a hell, so some would say I have dominion. If I make a big show of it, the Usurper will send bullies around. But if I lent you just a few companies of galla—"

"The galla might make all the difference."

"The three of you will come visit afterward?"

"Absolutely."

Ereshkigal gave a piercing whistle, and galla appeared in companies, unruly swarms of hundreds each. With snakes, with trident spears, with demon dogs whose black skin tore to show bones, sniggering like goblins, red and black and bone-pale, they came—some furry, some bare with burnt skin, some rotting, some dewy with blood, most with batlike wings, all stinking like a sewer full of rotting bodies. From them rose a hissing, buzzing sound, as if snakes and flies gave voice.

"Yessssssssss, missssssssssstressssssssssssss?"

"Consider this woman your queen until she returns you

to me. Do everything she says, without fail, and cause her no harm, or you will answer to me!"

"Yesssssssss, misssssssssstresssssssssssss."

The company turned to Joanie, a wash of eyes watching, bodies multitudinous in size, scaled skins and flat, reds and greys and blacks and muddy greens. She swallowed hard.

She could do this.

She bowed low before Ereshkigal, touching her lips to the dusty step before the throne. "My queen."

Ereshkigal's eyes glowed red.

"I do expect a visit from you and your friends when this is over."

"Of course."

Suddenly they were in the small side-building, a packed space. Joanie threw the door open. The galla poured out.

"Fight the white-winged ones! Support the darker angels and the incubus-succubus! Listen to the incubus-succubus —they're my co-captain!"

And then, as loud as she could, she shouted, "Puabi-Ekur! Azazel! Galla incoming!"

Chapter 56

In the night hospital, patches of light lay crossed by shadows on the pale blue-green of the wall and the white accordion screen. The smell of disinfectant hung in the air. A tube went into Joanie's arm, pumping her full of fluids.

"I thought she maybe did just have the flu," Gus whispered.

"They did a bunch of tests, but no one seems to know what it is," Cleo said. "Or if they do, they haven't said."

"We all know it's a spiritual battle reflected on this plane," Hannah said. "We can't know the outcome till it happens. But whatever's going on, we can ask Hekate for help."

Chapter 57

The galla surged forth. Ekur herded groups to Watchers, ordering them to follow the angels' commands. The galla's skill was torture.

Wielding trident spears, bat-winged galla worked white-feathered angels. Snakes bit, scorpions stung, lizard-headed monsters snatched and tore flesh and feathers. Occasionally a shout or a ululation burst from a dying angel.

Letting the galla distract Suriyel's followers, Ekur turned to the angel themself.

Suriyel confronted Azazel. Bit by bit, they were trying to cut him off from his company. Ekur took up his position at Azazel's back. Other dark angels joined them.

In a vicious dance, Ekur lunged, slashed, stabbed, looking for openings. These white wings were better fighters than the earlier ones. Yet galla and Watchers peeled angels away from Suriyel, dealing temporary death.

Azazel and Suriyel faced off. Ekur and another Watcher

fought those at Suriyel's side. Joanie stood in the doorway of the mudbrick side-building watching.

With a flash of silver, Suriyel blocked a thrust with their sickle sword.

A whisper rose above the tumult: "Call off your incubus and followers. Let us fight this out, angel to angel."

Suriyel's side was losing now. They wanted to fight one on one so earth nature would wear Azazel down.

"Don't do it," Ekur said, so only Azazel heard.

Azazel eyed him. To Suriyel, he yelled, "I shall not. Leave this space now, or die."

The shining silver-grey eyes glanced across the field of combat.

In a moment, all the heavenly angels except Suriyel winked out, like snuffed flames.

Spinning, Suriyel launched their sickle sword at Joanie.

It struck her through the forehead.

Chapter 58

Suriyel disappeared.

In the pocket hell, a wind moaned and died.

"Oh, no, no, no, no, no," said Ekur. "No, no, no."

Running to Joanie, he bent over her body. Azazel followed.

Her gaze had fixed. Blood dribbled from the red hole in her forehead. The sickle sword was gone.

"She will be with us as a spirit."

"It was not her time to die."

A breath of air shuffled dust.

"No one can die if it is not their time."

Azazel's angels looked from him to his companion and turned toward their tents, the wounded staggering, carried or half-carried by those more whole.

"You are an angel—you are outside of time. Retrieve her."

"That is a big request, succubus. I do not know if it is possible."

They stared at each other.

"I will put it before Hekate," Puabi-Ekur said.

In the deep heavens, among a scattering of stars, Puabi-Ekur lay, arms flung out. Past their shoulder ran the cloudy stellium called sometimes the Pale Cow's Path, sometimes the Way the Dog Ran, sometimes the Snake of the Skies—sometimes the Milky Way.

Before them stood the goddess's throne.

Time did not pass. They were outside time.

"I am yours, goddess. I am dedicated to your service. I've done your work—I've done it well. Grant me this wish."

They would wait in not-time all the ages of the world, if they had to.

At last, in a cloud of burned garlic, the Lady appeared.

"Rise, Puabi-Ekur. This is a nexus point."

They did not rise.

"Please," they begged.

"You ask for a different universe."

"Every change makes a different universe."

Puabi-Ekur looked up at the goddess, who before their eyes was young, then old, then young again.

"Please. You made me come back to myself. You knew then I'd have to care. I did everything you bid me. Please."

They began to cry, tears not of dust but of salt water.

The stars disappeared.

A wind moved across dust, scattering it to the sky.

Chapter 59

*P*uabi-Ekur found themselves hovering on the brink of the chasm in Dudael. The last blue-black wash of night hung above a glowing rose horizon.

On the wall of basalt, the chains hung empty.

As Puabi, they walked toward the black silk pavilion, from which a path of light fell among the brush. She moved toward the hillocks of black tents.

A whoosh and ping sounded.

As if erased, three-quarters of the tents disappeared.

A ray of light crossed her path, and a white-winged angel stood before her. Puabi drew herself together to change to Ekur.

But in their hands, the angel held an open book. Pages fluttered, showing hundreds of names, each crossed through with a line.

In a sonorous voice, the angel said, "Those who wished it among Azazel's legions are released."

When Puabi looked up, the angel was gone.

In the pavilion, she found Azazel in bed, black sheets pooled around him, not asleep but staring into nothingness. Bone-weary, she lay down beside him.

"Greetings, most fair."

"Beloved." Sitting up, she kissed his cheek. "The Demiurge freed your people. Their tents are gone."

He rolled off the bed. "I must see this."

In the dawn light, their shadows behind them, they took the scrub path.

"You are right."

Only a few dozen tents remained.

"I don't understand. The Demiurge lost a battle, not the war."

"This was not mercy. Freeing my company means I have fewer fighters."

"But it's what you wanted."

He kissed her forehead. "Yes. Now let us check the mortal plane."

Chapter 60

Joanie swam upward from sleep.

With a jolt, she realized she was in her bedroom at home. It shone white, sunlight reflected from silver threads and tiny mirrors on decorative pillows. The decor made her twitch—it would be a while before she could deal with so much white.

She sat up, rubbing her face, and grabbed her phone from the bedside table.

She pulled back in shock.

It had been a week since they did the ritual to free Azazel's legions.

She got up, took her robe from the hook on the door, wrapped herself into it, padded into the bathroom, used the toilet.

No sound in the house—Cleo must be out. It was a Thursday, midday.

She texted:

<What's up? Have I really been out a week?>

After only seconds, a text returned:

<You're awake! They said you were safe, so I went to work. You don't remember anything about the hospital?>

<The hospital?>

<I'll be home right away. Don't push yourself!>

She did feel tired, and woozy. When she stood a second time, her head spun. She went back to bed.

She woke to see her girlfriend staring at her from the end of the bed.

"My gods, you girl."

Cleo threw herself on her, which was un-Cleo-like behavior.

"What happened?"

"When you opened the door with the knife, there was a bang, like thunder. You fell down, stone cold passed-out. And your spirit-people were gone immediately."

"And since then?"

"You were on spirit journey, delirious, for days. We took you to the ER. Which was really lucky, because suddenly you were coughing. And then you fell. And then—" Cleo drew in a big breath. "Sweetheart, I think you died."

"Died?"

"Clinical death. Only for a moment. They had the defibrillator out immediately and restarted your heart. Then of course, they admitted you to the hospital. I just brought you home last night. You don't remember?"

Something had happened, something big. Her memories of the angel battles seemed continuous, but patched in somewhere was a blank space. When she tried to pin it down, it slipped away.

"How are we ever going to pay for the hospital?"

"We'll figure it out. We can do some kind of crowd-funding."

"How is Jeremy taking it?" Her coffee-shop boss.

"You know how he is. At first he was pissy. Once he got it was serious, though, he said take all the time you needed. It's not like you could have worked, anyway. You've been running a fever the whole time."

Cleo kissed her forehead, checking her temperature.

"You seem okay now. They never did put a name to what you had, at the hospital."

Sitting beside Joanie on the bed, she laid her palm to her cheek.

"We were so scared. What happened?"

"Let me tell you, it's been quite a fucking journey. First, I got kidnapped by angels."

Chapter 61

*I*n the pavilion, beside the bed of black silk, a few candles burned in the nearest candelabra. Puabi-Ekur, as Puabi, lay enfolded in Azazel's arms. They'd been drowsing.

The assignment was finished. Azazel was no longer Puabi-Ekur's boss. In the time since, Puabi-Ekur had visited often—half-lived there, if they were honest with themselves.

She sat up, shaking her mane of crimped black hair back from her face. Propped on one arm, she looked down at Azazel, his blue-grey eyes pale green in candlelight.

"A question," he said. "After my people were released, we found Saadiya recovering. A pleasant outcome. But do you remember begging Hekate to switch timelines?"

"What? No!"

He stroked her arm with his warm and callused palm.

"Let us say there was a timeline when that last shot from Suriyel hit Joanie and killed her. In that timeline, you went to Hekate and begged her to bring Joanie back."

"I don't remember that at all."

"The humans are saying she was clinically dead a few moments. But I remember both timelines."

Casting back, she caught an image of Suriyel throwing a sickle. She focused, and it disappeared, an eerie feeling. What had she lost?

"What else don't I remember?"

"I cannot know. For me, the difference is Saadiya."

She could try getting the full story out of Hekate, but that would go nowhere.

There were more present dangers. "Suriyel's still out there."

"All the Watchers know of the attack on us, even those who arrived too late to fight. Suriyel is barred by my comrades and may find themselves ambushed."

"There's no better solution?"

"Not against an immortal angel. On the other hand, you and Joanie have an immortal angel and his siblings to protect you."

Pulling her to his chest, Azazel caressed her hair, sending shivers through her. She relaxed into his hold.

"Hekate changed the timeline?"

"Never doubt the goddess listens to you, Puabi-Ekur."

Chapter 62

*J*oanie sat in her ritual room, staring at her coral-pink candle, with deep breaths calming herself into meditation.

A couple of weeks had passed since her brush with death. They'd scraped together some funds, between themselves and their community. Jeremy at the coffee shop had agreed to pay the rest—motivated by guilt, since he'd dragged his feet on providing employee insurance.

Though the candle was Inanna's, it surprised Joanie when the goddess popped into her meditation.

"My lady! I have missed you! I know I haven't been doing your work. Or maybe a little." Sex with Ereshkigal was a form of sacred whoredom, but Inanna might not think fucking her sister counted.

"An opportunity will come to you shortly. Be open!"

"I will!"

As quickly as she'd appeared, she left.

A few moments later, Joanie found herself in the black

silk pavilion in the pocket hell. Puabi-Ekur and Azazel lounged on the bed, the former in female form.

"Ereshkigal is asking after you," Puabi said.

"She did send the galla."

"I told her not to rush you—I said you almost died. She didn't take that very seriously."

"I'm ready to go if you are."

Maybe fucking Ereshkigal counted after all.

After the goddess's shout, the tussle of rolling limbs fell still. The four of them lay back panting in her vast bed, black sheets tumbled over the wood frame shining with gold and silver. Braziers wafted cypress and juniper smoke.

The goddess, as a Sumerian queen, lay with her gown discarded, crimped black hair falling over silky brown skin, dark areolae and nipples.

Joanie sat up, smoothing her tousled hair back behind her ears.

"Thank you again for your favors to us, bounteous lady."

"Thank you, beautiful one." The Lady reached out, stroked a finger down Joanie's breast, pinched her nipple. Joanie closed her eyes, giving in to the sensation.

"I feel fully paid for the loan of my galla. And yet I would enjoy seeing you all again. Feast with me, dance with me. Nergal's been asking about you."

That was her husband. What did Ereshkigal mean?

The goddess rolled her huge Sumerian eyes at Joanie's look. "Nergal takes an interest in my long-term lovers."

"My lady, I am honored." Also a little nervous—he was the god of plagues.

"We are honored," rumbled Azazel.

"Yes. Of course," Puabi-Ekur said, nudged by the angel. They'd manifested as male this time, to Ereshkigal's delight. He reached out and stroked Ereshkigal's ankle. "You know I will always come see you, if you desire."

The goddess pushed herself to sitting, rolling her shoulders.

"I fear I have duties now. The Annunaki gods wish to discuss details about judging humans. Every hell has its bureaucracy."

Leaning over, she kissed them each on the mouth in turn, the scent of sex mixing with cypress and juniper.

For Beltaine, Joanie got to Hannah's early, before Cleo, before the other coveners, friends, and guests.

In the backyard, lilacs bloomed, sentinels at the end of the property, leafed out in green hearts and covered in lavender cascades. In darkness, the moon rode among clouds and a few stars.

She stepped into the lilacs' embrace. Their heady scent filled the air; their leaves brushed her skin.

Behind her, with her, she felt Puabi-Ekur and Azazel.

Puabi-Ekur had been with her for years now, and yet it was different having them as a lover. Azazel had been a surprise—she'd never imagined connecting with a fallen angel. She'd always thought of herself as a pagan witch. She had to expand her self-definition now.

Their arms encircled her.

The sliding glass door to the backyard opened, and Alyssa stepped out—she lived here and must have been watching for Joanie.

Coming up, she hugged her, then took a half-step back.

"I'm so sorry. Cleo told me Moonshadow attacked you. They must have seen your connection to Azazel all along."

"How could you know?" Though she'd opened the door, which counted. "It's a warning to be careful."

"I should have talked to Hekate about them first, like Hannah said. I've banished them now and put up a bunch of wards."

Brushing back Alyssa's white-blonde hair, Joanie kissed her forehead.

"I hope it works."

They'd fought off Moonshadow—Suriyel—but the war between the Demiurge's angels and the Watchers was hardly over.

Had Moonshadow stopped spying?

"What if it doesn't work?" Alyssa asked.

"Then we'll push Moonshadow out again. But keep your eyes and ears open."

Other people were arriving, among them her beautiful Cleo. As Alyssa drifted over to meet Gus, Cleo crossed the yard to Joanie. Taking her in her arms, she kissed her.

Nora came out, trailed by her two remaining coven members. In the floodlight's glare, she looked worn. She was still running her farm with only one helper.

"I think we should move in with Nora when our lease is up," Joanie said.

"You sure?"

Living at the farm would mean a lot of driving, even if they made best use of the transit system. But if Joanie played her cards right, she might be able to quit her day job. Her erotic fan site had picked up—she was making more money on it than she ever had. If she worked with Inanna, things might improve still more. It was worth a try.

"It's what I've seen in vision. And your ancestors want you to farm. It just feels right."

They'd gotten to know Nora better over the course of the poison-path class. And Joanie's beloved Pete was connected to Nora's land.

"We'll have to talk it through with Hannah."

They planned to stay part of Hannah's coven. Hannah and Nora had once had issues—Joanie didn't want to tread on old jealousies.

"I think she'll get it."

The rest of Hannah's coven pushed through the sliding glass door into the yard. As coveners set up the altar, Gus sauntered over to Joanie and Cleo.

"I thought you might want to know, Julia caught me up on Odin's Hunt."

"What's up?"

"They're scared shitless. They're convinced we killed Max by hexing him. They're calling Odin to protect them. Since we're not doing any magic against them, they think it's working. I bet Odin's laughing at them."

Cleo frowned. "Maybe. But frightened people are dangerous."

"Jake is in charge now. He's more moderate. Also, people are getting disenchanted. The Hunt doesn't look good, scared and stupid and with Max gone. There aren't as many foot soldiers willing to do their bidding."

"I'm ready with my shotgun any time they want to come back," Cleo said.

Joanie raised an eyebrow. "It might be time to ask the private detective to take the next step. Talk to the Hunt guys who left—see if we can get a warrant to search for bones."

The ritual bell rang, calling the coven to circle.

Joanie crossed the grass, fingers interlaced with Cleo's. Puabi-Ekur and Azazel floated behind her. She took Gus's hand on her other side.

The scent of lilac hovered; the moon peered from between the clouds. A fog of moonlight covered the yard.

It gave her a start.

"That's not Moonshadow's aura, is it?"

Azazel gazed at the pale rays.

"I think not."

Moonlight glittered on the blade as Hannah raised her ritual knife to begin.

About the Author

Mary Trepanier writes fantasy, horror, and erotica. You can find her short stories in the *Blood in the Rain* anthologies of vampire erotica, among others. For more of *Tales of the End Times*, check out *The Queen of Heaven's Daughter, The Deer Stalker,* and *The Way to Witch Farm.*

Connect with Mary through her mailing list, her website (http://marytrepanier.com/),or by finding her on social media. Be the first to learn about each new volume in the *Tales of the End Times* series.